"You owe me for saving your life.

You told me so yourself. You called it something. A life present?"

Gage hadn't forgotten. The debt he owed Jenna had weighed heavily on his mind over the past weeks. He had every intention of returning the favor. Somehow. Someway. If he did not, he would suffer for all eternity, for his soul would not be permitted to cross over to the other side. However, he refused to believe that the gift would take the form of a wedding band.

"Life Gift," he corrected. "But you can't expect me to marry you."

"Do you owe me, Gage Dalton?"

Chagrin shot through him, and he knew she sensed it. And it only made her doggedness all the stronger.

"Are you going to pay your debt…or aren't you?"

Jenna Butler had him backed into a corner, and there wasn't a thing he could do about it.

Dear Reader,

What is the best gift you ever received? Chances are it came from a loved one and reflects to some degree the love you share. Or maybe the gift was something like a cruise or a trip to an exotic locale that raised the hope of finding romance and lasting love. Well, it's no different for this month's heroes and heroines, who will all receive special gifts that extend beyond the holiday season to provide a lifetime of happiness.

Karen Rose Smith starts off this month's offerings with *Twelfth Night Proposal* (#1794)—the final installment in the SHAKESPEARE IN LOVE continuity. Set during the holidays, the hero's love enables the plain-Jane heroine to become the glowing beauty she was always meant to be. In *The Dating Game* (#1795) by Shirley Jump, a package delivered to the wrong address lands the heroine on a reality dating show. Julianna Morris writes a memorable romance with *Meet Me under the Mistletoe* (#1796), in which the heroine ends up giving a widower the son he "lost" when his mother died. Finally, in Donna Clayton's stirring romance *Bound by Honor* (#1797), the heroine receives a "life present" when she saves the Native American hero's life.

When you're drawing up your New Year's resolutions, be sure to put reading Silhouette Romance right at the top. After all, it's the love these heroines discover that reminds us all of what truly matters most in life.

With all best wishes for the holidays and a happy and healthy 2006.

Ann Leslie Tuttle
Associate Senior Editor

Please address questions and book requests to:
Silhouette Reader Service
U.S.: 3010 Walden Ave., P.O. Box 1325, Buffalo, NY 14269
Canadian: P.O. Box 609, Fort Erie, Ont. L2A 5X3

DONNA CLAYTON

Bound by HONOR

SILHOUETTE *Romance* ®

Published by Silhouette Books

America's Publisher of Contemporary Romance

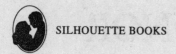 SILHOUETTE BOOKS

ISBN 0-373-19797-7

BOUND BY HONOR

This edition published by arrangement with Harlequin Books S.A.

® and TM are trademarks of Harlequin Books S.A., used under license.
Trademarks indicated with ® are registered in the United States Patent
and Trademark Office, the Canadian Trade Marks Office and in other
countries.

Visit Silhouette Books at www.eHarlequin.com

Printed in U.S.A.

Books by Donna Clayton

Silhouette Romance

Silhouette Books

The Coltons
Close Proximity

Logan's Legacy
Royal Seduction

*The Single Daddy Club
†Mother & Child
**Single Doctor Dads
††The Thunder Clan

DONNA CLAYTON

is a bestselling, award-winning author. She and her husband divide their time between homes in northern Delaware and Maryland's Eastern Shore. They have two sons. Donna also writes women's fiction as Donna Fasano.

Please write to Donna care of Silhouette Books. She'd love to hear from you!

Dear Reader,

I have long been interested in and captivated by Native American cultures, and I've done quite a bit of research that I've used in such books as *The Doctor's Medicine Woman, Close Proximity,* in my three-book series called THE THUNDER CLAN, and in this book, *Bound by Honor.*

Although many Native American tribes did not have a written language, they did have a strong oral tradition that kept (and continues to keep) their history vividly alive. Naturally, this custom touches the storyteller in me. I can easily imagine sitting in an intimate circle with family and friends while listening to dramatic tales of the past.

While doing some reading from my ever-growing reference library, I came upon an account of the belief in the Life Gift. If a person's life is saved by another, then that person owes a Life Gift—a debt that must be repaid. The idea intrigued me, and soon the plot of *Bound by Honor* began to take shape.

This book holds a special place in my heart. I hope you enjoy reading it as much as I enjoyed writing it.

Donna Clayton

Prologue

The wipers thumped furiously across the windshield. Jenna Butler leaned forward, straining to see the narrow road through the thick curtain of driving rain. Her knuckles were white against the gray steering wheel, every muscle in her body stiff. Worry and fear ripped at her gut.

Amy *had* to be okay. Jenna refused to consider any notion other than arriving at the hospital to find her sister bright-eyed and chattering away as usual. The harried E.R. nurse who had called from Deaconess Hospital offered little in the way of information, only notifying Jenna of the auto accident and urging her to come to the hospital as soon as the storm subsided.

Spring always brought rain to the southern plains of Montana, but storms of this magnitude were rare. Black clouds billowed and ill-omened thunder rolled across the sky. However, bad weather couldn't keep Jenna from Amy, not if her sister had been shaken up…or hurt…or worse.

Panic chilled her to the bone. *No!* Jenna wouldn't think that way. Amy was fine. She was healthy, and whole, and fine.

Jenna repeated the silent chant as the car crested a small rise in the road. Her spine went rigid when she registered the danger that awaited her directly ahead. She stomped on the brake pedal. The tires squealed in protest, and the back end of the car fishtailed. Jenna's heart hammered. A scream gathered at the back of her throat, but it died when the tires grabbed the blacktop and the car came to a sudden, jerky halt.

Inhaling a ragged breath, she blinked, realizing that she was staring at a field of sodden wheat. Luckily, she was still on the asphalt, but her car straddled both lanes, perpendicular to oncoming traffic. The wipers slapped a rhythmic tune, the engine purred, rain battered the roof in a torrent. She looked to her left and saw the sloped road from where she'd come. To her right, she saw the water. That wasn't just water, she realized. It was a river. A flash flood had washed out Reservation Road.

It was too late to regret not having taken the highway. Getting to the hospital in Billings as quickly as possible had been Jenna's only thought, so she'd taken the shortest route, the one that cut through Broken Bow Reservation. She pounded the steering wheel in frustration.

Lights in her peripheral vision drew her attention. The water coursing down the window distorted her view, but there was no mistaking the pickup that was racing over the small ridge in the road. The driver didn't slow down, but headed straight for her. Adrenaline surged. If she pulled her car forward to avoid a collision, the approaching driver might plunge headlong into the floodwaters roiling across the washed-out road.

Without hesitation, she shoved open her door. Fat raindrops pelted her full in the face as she bolted from the car, waving her arms frantically.

Rubber screeched against the wet pavement and the battered truck spun in a circle before skidding onto the narrow strip of weedy mud that separated the roadway from the wheat field. Stunned, Jenna shoved her hair from her face and raced to the truck. The handle felt icy against her fingertips as she pulled open the driver's side door.

"Are you all right?" Even as the question burst from her lips, she could see the trickle of blood oozing from a small cut on the man's temple. Her voice lowered to a whisper. "Oh, Lord, you're hurt."

He looked up at her then, and Jenna felt as if a rumble of stormy thunder had shuddered through her being. Never had she seen eyes so black. Like chips of polished onyx. His fierce gaze seemed to latch onto her, connect with something deep within, tug at her very soul.

Jenna swallowed. Suppressed the shiver that threatened to jolt through her. And then she took a tentative backward step.

What was the matter with her? Whimsy had never had a place in her thought processes. Romanticism was Amy's department. Jenna was logical. Rational. Suddenly, she understood. She was running on pure, high-octane nervous energy.

"I-is anything broken?" she stammered. "Can you move?"

The man had the high, regal cheekbones and swarthy complexion distinctive of Native American ancestry. She had no choice but to admit that he was handsome. He was more than merely handsome. Striking would be a better word to describe him.

Again, she was astounded by his eyes. Black orbs that seared into her like laser beams. Suddenly, she had the thought that she should do or say something before she fell headlong into his inscrutable gaze.

Tilting her head a fraction, she carefully enunciated, "Are you able to respond? Can you hear me?"

His sharp features grew taut with obvious annoyance. *Great,* Jenna thought. Dealing with an angry man was the last thing she needed.

"Of course, I can hear you." Accusation honed his tone to flint. "I could have run you over. What the hell are you doing in the middle of the road?"

Saving your lousy neck, she wanted to snap at him, but didn't. Instead, she stood there with rain running down her face in rivulets, soaking through her clothes until they were plastered to her skin, and explained, "Porcupine Creek overflowed its banks. The road's washed out. I nearly drove into it myself."

Seemingly unmindful of the downpour, the man shoved himself from his truck and stalked up the road far enough to view for himself the flood churning and swirling as it raced across the yawning gap in the asphalt. She wondered if he hadn't believed her when she told him why she'd flagged him down. What did he think? That she made a habit of standing out in the rain to direct traffic during every storm that swept across the great state of Montana?

As perturbed as she was, Jenna realized she couldn't take her eyes off him. His shoulders were broad and muscular beneath his wet denim shirt, clear evidence that, whatever he did for a living, he worked hard. Rain saturated his long hair, turning it to a slick, black river that coursed down his back. He certainly was solid. Well built. A stone wall of a man…with granite for a brain, no doubt. She parted her lips to speak again, and tasted the sweet, cool rainwater on her tongue. Shaking her head, she forced herself into action, walking forward until she was beside him.

"It's obvious that Kit-tan-it-to'wet had plans for me today," he murmured. "Plans to bring relief." His black eyes raked over her.

For the merest fraction of a second, she considered how she must look. Surely, the pelting rain had smeared her mascara. With raccoon eyes and her hair plastered to her head, she must be a frightful sight to behold.

The man seemed oblivious to her appearance, though, as he charged, "You changed my path."

Jenna squared her shoulders. She didn't like his tone. She had no idea what he was talking about, but a person could only take so much insolence before losing it.

"I don't know why you would be angry," she snapped. "Anyone with an ounce of intellect could see that I saved your butt. I kept you from driving into *that*." She pointed at the dangerous waters.

Evidently unimpressed, he only stared at her, his

jaw muscle ticking. Finally, he choked out, "Not only did you change my path, but now I am indebted to you. I owe you a Life Gift. One that I am obliged to repay."

His gaze was as stormy as the sky overhead, and that completely baffled her.

"You don't owe me anything," she stated with as much patience as she could muster. "I did what any decent human being would do. I narrowly avoided a dangerous catastrophe, and I did what I could to see that you avoided it, too. Let's not blow this out of proportion."

Amy. David. The accident. Deaconess Hospital. Like sparks flashing in the darkness, the thoughts rose to the forefront of her mind.

"Look, I've got to go," she told him. Her gaze darted to the cut on his temple. She saw that an angry lump had risen there. "I'm on my way to Billings. To the hospital. I could take you there. To see a doctor about that—"

With the speed of a bolt of lightning, he grasped her forearm. "I'm not going anywhere. And neither are you. I don't know who you are, or where I can find you…"

He stopped speaking suddenly, apparently sensing her fear. He released his hold on her arm. Common sense told Jenna she should flee from this stranger who had put his hands on her, but she watched his tongue trace his bottom lip, whisking away the rainwater, and she felt something akin to static electricity dance along her nerve endings. Goose bumps rose on her arms.

"I'm sorry," he said. "I don't blame you for being leery. I had no right to do that."

His tone was softer now, but he didn't smile. Jenna

got the distinct impression that smiling wasn't something that came easily for him.

"You don't know me," he continued, his words rolling faster from that wide, beautiful mouth.

Beautiful? The observation nearly shocked a gasp from her. *Jenna, hon,* a silent voice screamed in her head, *anxiety over Amy has driven you halfway to the loony bin.*

"Let me try to rectify that. I'm Gage. Gage Dalton. And I live here on the rez. On Broken Bow Reservation. I was on my way to Billings. To meet someone."

He was attempting to put her at ease; however, some self-preserving instinct told her to get away from him. Now. However, something else inside her—something bone-deep—was calling for her to stay, to listen to his explanation, which only frightened her more.

"I have to go," she stressed, swiping the moisture from her face and backing away. "There's been an emergency. My sister—"

Alarm cut off her words and widened her eyes when he reached out to once again halt her retreat. But he caught himself, balled his hand into a fist and lowered it to his side without touching her. "I mean you no harm." Then he did the most extraordinary thing. He splayed his palm against his chest, right over his heart. A pledge.

Although the fear pulsing through her subsided, the urgent need to get to Amy swelled like the floodwaters of Porcupine Creek.

Without knowing exactly why, she whispered, "Jenna. My name's Jenna Butler. I really do have to go."

His desperation seemed to hum like a silent tune. She knew she should be on her way. Amy needed her. But Jenna simply couldn't get the muscles of her legs to obey her frantic commands.

"Look—" his black brows inched together "—it would be impossible for me to make you understand what…to understand my beliefs. But I cannot—" He stopped. His corded throat convulsed in a swallow. "Owing a Life Gift is—" Again, he halted. "I *must* repay you in some way."

Getting to Amy was Jenna's only thought now. The swollen creek had cost her precious time. She would have to backtrack nearly ten miles to get to the interstate.

"I really don't have time for this. I've already told you that you owe me nothing."

Irritation flickered in his taut features. "It doesn't matter what you think I do or do not owe."

A whispery thought floated at the fringes of her brain, telling her she should feel insulted by his blunt words, but then a sudden and desperate idea flashed in her head. "There *is* something you could do. Say a prayer that my sister, Amy, is okay."

With that, she turned on her heel and made a mad dash for her car. She got in, jammed the engine into gear and got herself turned in the right direction. As she sped back toward the rise in the road, she glanced in the rearview mirror at the tall Native American standing in the pouring rain.

Chapter One

Two months later

"This is absolutely insane." However, the murmured opinion didn't discourage the determination in her step as she tramped across the neatly trimmed grass between the house and the gravel drive. "The man is not going to help you. He probably won't even *remember* you."

Normal, everyday behavior for Jenna didn't customarily include talking to herself. But her life had been anything but normal over the course of the past eight weeks. Thick emotion threatened to consume her when she contemplated all she'd endured, all she continued to endure; the sadness, the grief, the overwhelming frustration of dealing with the Lenape Council of Elders. So she thrust the thoughts from her mind and, instead, focused on the reason she'd come to Broken Bow—finding a solution to her problem.

Yes, coming here might be crazy. And, yes, once she presented her proposition, the man might laugh her into next week. But she'd turned the situation over in her head every which way, and this was the only answer she'd come up with.

The plain plank steps leading to the door of the rustic but contemporary ranch were sturdy under her feet. The covered porch offered a shady respite from the sweltering summer sun. The house was built with rough-hewn timber. Lifting her hand, she rapped on the door before anxiety stole away her nerve.

During the past weeks, the reservation had become a familiar place to her…a place filled with little more than apprehension and defeat. When the idea of garnering the help of Gage Dalton had popped into her head several days ago, she'd begun asking around about him.

However, as hard as she'd tried, she'd been unsuccessful in getting anyone to talk about him. What little information she had been able to gather about the man had left her feeling extremely unsure as to whether she should even attempt to approach him. But she simply had to do something.

Jenna hated feeling desperate, but that was exactly how she *and* her circumstances could be described. If he turned his back on her, she didn't know what she would do.

When he didn't answer the door, unexpected relief swept through her.

"Get in your car and drive away," she muttered under her breath. But instead of listening to reason, she reached up and knocked again. This time even harder. A mocking voice inside her head warned once again that this scheme was utterly outrageous.

The house showed no sign of life.

Dalton pretty much keeps to himself.

Rarely leaves his ranch.

Prefers to be left alone.

Those were the few pieces of information Jenna had accumulated while trying to locate Gage Dalton. Those who had talked to her had made him sound like some kind of hermit. And each and every person she'd approached, whether they offered information or not, had cast a peculiar glance, obviously wondering why she was searching for the man, but thankfully they'd been too polite to probe.

At a nearby service station, the talkative teenage boy who had checked her car's oil had commented, "We haven't seen much of Gage for the past year." Then he'd offered the most curious clue of all when he'd added, "The accident changed him."

Although she'd wanted to query further, other customers had occupied the boy's attention.

She should have taken the teen's words as a warning. Put together with her own tense experience with the man the tragic day of that horrendous storm, she should be running for the high hills, not seeking him out with a request for what was sure to be an awesome benevolence, *if* he agreed to help her. Doubt reared its head, hissing like an ugly snake, but she refused to surrender. She wouldn't—*couldn't*—back away from this. She had too much at stake.

Gage Dalton was her only hope. Her only chance of getting what she wanted.

The people of Broken Bow had inferred that Gage was an island—a lone and wounded man who kept himself isolated from the world. Well, he couldn't avoid her. She meant to see him.

"Gage Dalton!"

Several birds in the treetops were startled into flight.

She descended the porch steps and rounded the corner of the house. To her surprise, she saw a fenced paddock where two black-and-white horses moseyed about. There were several outbuildings, as well as a large stable located down a short, dusty lane.

The property was substantial, she realized, amazed she hadn't observed its size as she'd approached the house in her car. She turned, her gaze scanning the hard-packed, winding gravel drive. Fences spanned as far as she could see, and more horses grazed in one of several enclosed meadows. She'd seen enough western movies to identify those horses. Gage Dalton bred pintos.

She called, "Hello!"

He stepped into her view, stopping in the open double doors of the stable. Shirtless, he clasped a metal rake in one hand.

Her eyes cruised down the length of him. Sunlight gleamed against his bronze chest. Abdominal muscles rippled all the way down to the worn blue jeans that rode low on his trim waist and hugged his thighs. She dragged her gaze back up to his face. Those black eyes homed in on her, making her feel as if the very air around her had constricted. Even though he must have been nearly fifty yards away, she could sense the same tense displeasure pulsing from him as she'd felt the terrible, stormy day when they'd first met. Clearly, he hadn't been expecting a visitor, nor was he happy to see one.

The sight of him impelled her to turn tail and run. But thoughts of little Lily whispered through her mind, prompting Jenna to stand her ground. Her motive for being here was all-important. Even the formidable Gage Dalton couldn't keep her from getting what she wanted.

Well, he *could*. But she planned to do everything in her power to see that he didn't.

Ignoring his unwelcoming countenance, Jenna trudged toward him. She hoped her cheery smile hid the emotions warring inside her.

The closer her steps brought her to him, the heavier her doubt about his help grew.

A soft summer breeze fluttered the ends of his long hair.

"Hello, there." She was pleased that her greeting came out so smoothly. But then the stammering started. "I—I was a little wet and disheveled w-when we last m-met…and it's been weeks ago…so…well…I don't know if you remember me, but—"

"Jenna Butler."

Her shoulders relaxed as relief soothed the anxiety that provoked the awkward song and dance she'd just performed. Without thought, she softened her tone to nearly a whisper and murmured, "Oh, good. You do remember."

The seconds ticking by felt like eons as the warm sunshine beat down on her head and shoulders. Finally, he shifted his grip on the wooden pole, planting the rake's prongs into the ground. The impatience in the gesture had her nervousness sprouting to life all over again.

Jenna had known the task at hand was going to be tough, but she hadn't realized just how tough. Now that she was face-to-face with Gage Dalton and about to ask an awesome favor…why, she couldn't remember a time when she'd felt more ill at ease.

"H-how are you?" she blurted. "You hit your head during the accident, I remember."

"I'm alive."

She couldn't read much from his deadpan expression. Feeling the need to infuse some amiability between them, she chuckled. "That's good. Sure beats the alternative."

Her humor seemed lost on him.

Grasping for something more to break the ice, she looked around her, commenting, "You've got a nice place here."

"I like it."

So he wasn't much of a talker. She should have guessed as much, judging from what she'd learned of him. But it sure would be nice if she didn't have to work so hard.

She had to warm things up a little before broaching the favor she needed from him. If she just blurted out her question, cold turkey, he'd think she was insane.

Jenna, my girl, a voice in her head groaned silently, *you* are *insane.*

She tried again. "The horses are beautiful." Glancing over at the animals in the pen, she added, "I've never spent much time around horses, but I know those are pintos from the old cowboy movies I watched as a kid. They sure are majestic-looking creatures. Proud. Untouchable. They might be enclosed, but they sure do look wild."

As if on cue, one of the horses snorted and clawed at the dusty ground with his hoof.

"They're tame," he assured her. "What you see is attitude. If a horse is broken to the point that it's docile, it's no better than a pack mule. My horses are intelligent and strong and spirited."

Seemed Gage Dalton possessed a healthy share of attitude himself. Life sparked in his onyx eyes as he talked about the animals he raised. Then he leveled his gaze on her.

"Is that why you're here? You're interested in a pinto?"

The question elicited another chuckle from her, this one completely natural. "Oh, no," she told him. "Not me. I wouldn't know one end of a horse from the other."

She couldn't tell if the tiny crease that suddenly marred his high brow was a sign of curiosity or suspicion. He glanced down at the ground, tapped the rake absently with his foot, and then lifted his chin to meet her gaze.

"Well, you've found out that I weathered the accident just fine," he said. "And you've complimented my ranch. And my horses. We could talk about the weather, if you like. Or how rising gasoline prices are thinning our wallets. But I'd prefer it if we cut the small talk. I have stalls to muck before I can stable those horses. Why don't you save us both some time and tell me why you're here?"

The blunt question left her momentarily speechless. But then, before she'd even had time to think, words began tumbling off her tongue.

"My sister died. The day of the storm. The day you and I met on the road. I remember telling you I was on my way to the hospital." Anguish gathered in a tight ball high in her chest. "Her husband was killed, too. They…they ran off the road. The car flipped. Into a ravine. My brother-in-law died instantly. Amy…my sister…sh-she held on for several hours." The emotion rose to knot in her throat. It became so overwhelming that she had to glance toward the horizon as she whispered, "But she passed soon after I reached the hospital."

Jenna blinked back the tears that burned her eyes. She would not cry. She didn't know this man, refused to show her vulnerability to him. He had to know her story, though. Otherwise, how could he understand her plight? The tribal council had forced her into a desperate situation, and that was the only reason she was here. But Gage Dalton must not see her as weak. Because she wasn't.

It was the stark silence that drew her from her thoughts. Why didn't he say something? What kind of person didn't offer condolences after learning about a death in the family? In this case, two deaths.

Her gaze clashed with Gage's, and the sentiment clouding his eyes shocked her. Sympathy rolled off him in waves. He didn't have to say a word; everything he felt was expressed in those soft black orbs.

The muscle in the back of his jaw went taut, and he

seemed to be engaged in a mental struggle of some sort. His tone was tight, his words grating, when he finally spoke.

"I know grief well." He swallowed.

His keen, too-intense focus on her made her feel as if she were the only person alive on Earth at that moment.

"May your heart find healing."

Of all the cards and letters, flowers and prayers she'd received from friends and business acquaintances since losing Amy and David, Jenna couldn't recall a more comforting wish. She found his words both simple and beautiful. Abundantly so.

Hot tears made a fresh attack, but she blinked them back. She still had a great deal to explain before she could broach the sensitive subject of why she'd come to him for help. Losing herself in sorrow was something she couldn't afford to do.

"Thank you," she murmured, her breath hitching between the two short words. Willing a vibrant potency into her voice, she repeated, "Thank you very much."

Another gust of warm summer wind blew across the Montana prairie lands. The sun high overhead continued to heat her shoulders and back through her light cotton top. Slowly, she was able to push the sorrow at bay and latch onto the resolve that had brought her here in the first place.

"Amy was married to a Lenape Indian who lived on Broken Bow," Jenna told Gage. "David Collins was his name."

"The artist?" Gage propped the metal rake he'd been holding against the stable door. "I knew he lived on the rez, even met him a couple of times. I've seen some of his work. Very abstract-looking. Canvases that incorporate paint as well as three-dimensional material."

"It's called mixed media."

"He's very talented." His tone lowered an octave as he said, "I guess I should say *was*. He signed his works Foxfire, didn't he?"

Jenna nodded.

Gage continued, "I think I read somewhere that his wife was an artist, too."

Jenna nodded. "Amy was a painter. She met David in Chicago when she attended a showing of his work. They got married shortly thereafter."

Gage shook his head. "I hadn't heard about the accident."

From what she'd learned of this man's solitary existence, Jenna wasn't surprised.

"They left behind a baby," she told him. "Lily. My niece. She's just over six months old."

Emotion softened the harsh angles of his handsome face. Could that be sadness?

His reaction took Jenna aback. She hadn't expected his compassion. Not at all. She'd anticipated he would be completely unemotional. Relieved that she'd been wrong, she hoped his empathy might impel him to help her.

Reaching up, she tucked a wayward strand of hair behind her ear before she spoke again. "The night of the accident, Lily had been with David's parents. I thank God every day that Lily wasn't in that car. Health problems make it impossible for Mr. and Mrs. Collins to care for my niece, so she's been staying with a sitter here on the reservation. A woman named Arlene Johnson. I went to collect Lily, but Arlene refused to allow me to take Lily home with me. Arlene said I'd have to get permission from the Council. I had no idea at the time what she was talking about. Amy and David left no will. But I'm family. I didn't need anyone's permission but the state of Montana's to take custody of my niece.

"A lawyer in Billings told me he couldn't help me," she continued. "He said the residents of Broken Bow aren't held accountable to the laws of the United States. That Native Americans govern themselves. That I would be at the mercy of the Council of Elders overseeing the tribe." Her voice went hoarse as she added, "He didn't offer me much hope of getting Lily."

Gage's chin tipped up a fraction. "Everything you were told is true. We are managed by the Elders. There are eight men and women on our—"

"I know. I've met them." Her response was flat, but she couldn't help it. Those people had made the past eight weeks of her life utterly miserable.

Evidently, he took exception to the impudent implication in her tone. He crossed his arms over his broad chest, and she wondered just how hard his pecs might feel beneath her fingertips.

Gage shifted his weight.

"I'm sorry," she murmured, embarrassed by her inability to suppress her feelings about the Elders—but probably more so that she'd become too aware of his physique.

She looked him in the eye. "I don't mean any disrespect. Honestly, I don't. It's just that…well, I've spent the past two months feeling terribly frustrated. I've done everything the Council has asked of me. I've answered a battery of questions. I've opened myself completely. Revealed my past. My present. My dreams for the future. I've confessed that I've spent my whole life building my e-commerce business, maybe to my own detriment since I have no husband or children of my own. I've revealed my financial situation. I've proved that building commercial Web sites is profitable. I've submitted to a physical. I've laid out my philosophy of life. I've told them all they want to know. I've pleaded with them. Told them that I'm willing to change my whole life in order to raise Lily. Explained that losing Amy and David has opened my eyes to what family means. I begged them, Gage, during meeting after meeting. For two long months. Yet they continue to thwart me at every turn." Her tone grew nearly frantic. "I need some help. I need an ally. And I need one now."

Suddenly, the sympathy Gage had shown for her situation seemed to have evaporated like morning dew under the heat of the sun. At some point during her explanation of her dealings with the Elders of his tribe—she couldn't say exactly when—his entire body had gone rigid.

He'd transformed back into the hard-hearted man she'd met the day of the storm. *This* was the response she'd been expecting when she first thought to seek him out.

"The only reason you came here," he accused, "is because I'm Indian. You think I can influence the Council in some way."

Nearby, she heard one of the horses whinny. She

didn't dare break eye contact with Gage. Doing so would send the message that she was somehow ashamed of coming here.

Well, she wasn't ashamed. Obtaining custody of Lily was her only concern. And she'd face a bevy of Councils to get what she wanted. She'd face one angry Lenape Indian, too.

Her niece needed her. And Jenna needed to raise her sister's baby.

An ache wrenched her heart when she pondered the notion of forever losing the guardianship of Lily. But Jenna swallowed the pain. She had a cause to plead. And she'd better come up with a damned good argument.

She squared her shoulders. "I'm not going to lie to you, Gage," she began quietly. "I *am* here because you're Native American. Lenape, specifically. David was the only man from Broken Bow that I knew. I've done some work for Cheyenne-owned businesses. But I don't know any of those people well enough to ask for their help now."

"And you know me?"

"No. No, I don't. But I'm desperate, Gage. One of the reasons the Council won't let me have Lily is because I'm white. I might not like the position I find myself in, but I need help from someone of Native American ancestry. Someone from the Lenape tribe. Someone from Broken Bow. And you fit all those criteria."

His expression turned stormy, and Jenna began to feel the first pangs of hopelessness. But she plowed ahead. "Lily and I need to be together. That baby is all I have left of Amy and David. I'm the only maternal relative Lily's got left. And David's parents aren't able to care for her. Like I said, they haven't been keeping Lily. She's been living with the sitter, for goodness' sake!"

Despite her determination not to look weak, utter frustration made her eyes well. A huge, watery tear rolled down her face. Feeling it tickle her skin, she lifted her hand and dashed it away.

"Please try to understand," she whispered. *"I love that baby!"*

The muscles in his jaw constricted. Reaching up, he rubbed his hand over his chin, then scrubbed the back of his neck, his gaze drifting off toward the horizon.

Finally, he turned his gaze to her again. "Jenna, it's not that I don't want to help you. It's just that…" He shook his head and looked away again, dragging his fingers through his long, glossy hair.

His hesitation lifted her spirits the merest fraction. Was there a chance she could make her plan come to fruition? Was there a chance she'd made him grasp the gravity of her situation?

Gage moistened his lips then, riveting Jenna's gaze to his mouth. She wondered about his kiss. Would it be searing? Would it be sweet? Would it be soft?

A strange current danced through her. She closed her eyes, inhaled deeply through her nose, exhaled through her mouth. Anxiety was wreaking havoc on her nervous system, making her entertain the most peculiar thoughts.

"Look, Jenna."

The intensity of his black eyes jolted her.

"I just don't see how I can help you. I do understand that you need someone to do something. You need someone—an Indian—to plead your case to the Council. You need someone to stand up for you. But this doesn't have anything to do with me. It's none of my business." He pressed his palm flat against his chest. "I'd give you a character reference. But I don't even know you."

Oh, God. He was turning her down. Misery sank in her gut like a lead weight.

"It's not a character reference I need, Gage." She might as well come completely clean. What could it hurt at this point? "As I told you, one of the reasons the Council won't let me have Lily is because I'm white. The other reason is because I'm single."

Confusion knit his brow. Jenna bit back a frustrated sigh. He still wasn't getting it. She was going to have to spell it out.

"What I *need*—" she spoke slowly and succinctly, "—is a *husband*."

Chapter Two

Gage gaped at the woman standing before him. Staring was rude. His parents had taught him that long ago. But he couldn't help it. The request Jenna Butler had made shocked the words right out of him and made him forget good manners.

"You're looking at me like I'm nuts," she said. "My idea isn't all that crazy, you know."

Nuts. Crazy. Perfect adjectives to describe her *and* her suggestion.

"For weeks, the Council has used my ethnicity as an excuse for why I can't have Lily."

Nervous agitation had her clenching and unclenching her fists. Gage could tell she wasn't even aware she was doing it.

"I met with them last week. And that's when they

claimed that if I were to take her from Broken Bow," she continued, "and raise her in the 'white world,' as they put it, that Lily would lose touch with her Native American heritage, that she'd forget who she is and where she came from. That she'd forget she was Delaware. I promised them I wouldn't let that happen. But evidently, they don't believe me."

Gage's gaze strayed over her lovely face. Her features were delicate—gracefully arched eyebrows, thick lashes framing almond-shaped eyes, a pert little nose. Her pale skin glowed with the iridescence of moonlight, fresh and shimmery. The noonday sun burnished her shoulder-length auburn hair, the ends curling softly and resting against the topmost part of her full, rounded breasts.

Awareness tightened deep in his belly and made his mouth go dry. Gage frowned. Admiring this woman's body was the *last* thing he should be doing. He forced his gaze back to her face and immediately noticed that her eyes were doe-brown, soft and dewy. Shadowy half circles smudged the skin beneath them, evidence that she'd spent many a sleepless night wrestling with her problem.

"Finally, I became so frustrated that I lost my temper," she continued. "I reminded them all that Lily was half white. I told them that it was wrong to keep me from raising my niece because of my race."

His brows rose heavenward. Customarily, deeming what was right and wrong was the job of the Elders, not those who stood before them.

"I told them that I loved that baby, and that I would

treat her as my own. Gage, she *is* my own. I was so angry. My tongue got away from me. I blurted out that if they didn't give me custody of Lily, that it would be a sin. One that they would have to answer for."

He imagined the Council receiving a good dressing-down from this woman and a smile tugged at the corners of his mouth. Luckily, he wrestled it under control.

Jenna Butler was a fighter. That much was undeniable.

"How did the Elders respond?"

Fire sparked in her eyes. "They called a halt to the meeting, then and there. I phoned every day for nearly a week. I thought I'd lose my mind. Finally, they agreed to see me again. Just yesterday. That's when I discovered their trumped-up concern that I was single and unable to give Lily a stable upbringing."

She shook her head in aggravation, her hair brushing those luscious mounds of—

Gage cut his eyes to the ground, studying the toes of his dusty work boots.

"It's not fair, Gage. And it's not right! I'm not going to let them do this to me. Or to Lily."

He couldn't help but admire her determination and strength. She had a will of iron. That was good. Going head-to-head with the Council, she would certainly need it.

Her chin tipped upward. "I don't want to lower myself to begging. But if that's what it will take to get you to help me, then I will. Please, Gage, I need you."

What the hell could he possibly say to this woman?

Reaching behind him, he pulled a kerchief from his back pocket and swiped it across his brow. Not that he was hot or perspiring. He was stalling for time. He needed to think. He needed to come up with some way to let Jenna Butler down easy.

"Gage."

Something in the way she said his name eased the tension in him.

"Please."

"Look," he began, "there's a big difference between asking for my help and asking me to—"

His throat caught, making it impossible for him to voice the words he never thought he'd utter again.

"Marry me," she supplied. "I'm asking you to marry me, Gage, so that I can get custody of Lily. If you'll do this for me, the Council can't possibly refuse me. Their excuses will be worthless. For I'll no longer be single, and my husband will be Delaware."

Great Spirit above! She presented her plan as if it were a completely logical course of action.

"You're asking me to deceive the Elders of my tribe." He bunched the handkerchief in his palm. "If they discover that I'm helping you trick them, they could force me to leave Broken Bow."

Such drastic action hadn't been taken for generations, as far as he knew; however, the possibility remained.

Surprise momentarily slackened her jaw. "I hadn't realized that." Instantly, her resolve sparked anew. "But I won't let that happen, Gage. I promise you, I won't."

Although he'd had his share of run-ins with the Council, he felt the need to speak up for his leaders now. "They're not looking to torture you, Jenna. Their number one priority is your niece's best interest. You have to understand that. Priority number two is the tribe. David Collins's daughter is considered by the Elders to be Delaware. It doesn't matter that her mother was white. The child is Indian. She is an important part of the tribal clan. Think of it as an extended family. The Delaware family. The child—"

"The child's name—" ire tightened her facial muscles "—is Lily. And she's got Butler blood running through her, too. She might be an important part of your tribe, but she's the only family I have left."

Anger evidently got the better of her, and with her fists balled, she dug her toe into the dirt. A tiny tuft of dust billowed and then settled over her white canvas sneaker.

"You're spouting off the same hogwash that the Council has been giving me for weeks."

The woman's steel was to be admired, but she was also beginning to annoy him. "You have no idea just how serious the Elders are about their responsibilities to this tribe."

Defeat rounded her shoulders. "I'm terribly sorry, Gage," she said. "I never meant to…"

She didn't finish her sentence. Tilting her chin sharply, she looked at the sky, exhaled and then swallowed. Gage couldn't help but notice the elegant length of her throat. Again, he dragged his attention to her face, but found himself enthralled with the ripeness of her mouth—full, moist lips that promised passion. Her kiss would taste as sweet as wild honey, he was sure.

Irritation churned in his gut as he remembered being assaulted with the exact same thought the day of the storm. The first time they'd met. That day, rainwater had streamed down her face, making her coral-colored lips glisten with tantalizing wetness. How many nights since then had he dreamed about suckling the moisture from them? Like an elusive wraith, she had haunted his sleep for weeks. He never knew when she would appear in his dreams, and when she did, he always awakened in a sweat, yearning and need pulsing through his body.

His indignation smoldered. However, his anger wasn't directed at her, but at himself. Why wasn't he able to control his own mind? His own flesh? These damnable carnal thoughts?

He'd concluded that his anxiety was the cause, that he was being plagued by the dreams because he was worrying about repaying the woman what he owed. However, why the night fantasies would take on such an erotic tone continued to confuse him.

"Losing Amy and David has been so hard," she whispered. "And not being able to have Lily with me has been…well, it's been like losing my entire family."

Moisture made her brown eyes shine, and a tear rolled down her milky cheek. He experienced the most peculiar reaction. He wanted to comfort her. To reach out and wipe away that tear. To offer the solution she so desperately searched for.

What the hell? Had he lost his mind? Was he honestly contemplating her crazy scheme?

No! a voice in his head shouted. A union such as the one this woman was suggesting would make a mockery of the marriage he'd had—and lost. A loving union that had ended much too soon.

Marrying Jenna Butler would denigrate the memory of the woman he'd loved. The woman he continued to mourn.

Taking sacred vows that would tie him to a complete stranger in order that she might obtain custody of a baby would disrespect the infant daughter he'd lost so tragically…a child for whom Gage grieved every day of his miserable life.

"I'm sorry." Emotion swam in the pit of his gut, hazed his thinking. But he fought to remain resolute. "Jenna, I understand your pain. More than you realize." The lump that had swelled in his throat made it difficult to breathe. "But I cannot help you."

Her chin trembled, and Gage had to force himself not to look away from the heartbreak expressed on her angelic face. He couldn't let her tears affect him. He braced himself by gritting his teeth so tightly that a dull ache began to pulsate in the joints of his jaw.

"You *can't?* Or you *won't?*"

"What does it matter? I refuse to participate in your foolish plan. You cannot dupe the Council into handing over your niece. You try, and they'll forbid you from having any contact with her."

Jenna's eyes went wide. "They can't do that."

"They can. And they will, if they come to the conclusion that that's what's best for your niece. They are the law on Broken Bow."

Suddenly, her resolve crumbled. She buried her face in her hands, her shoulders shaking with soft sobs. Discomfited, Gage stuffed his hands deep into the pockets of his jeans. He sympathized with her, but there was nothing he could do.

"You owe me!" she exclaimed, jerking up her head to glare at him as she dashed at her tears. "You told me so yourself. You owe me for saving your life that day the storm washed out Reservation Road. You called it something. A present. Wasn't it? A life present?"

Of course, he hadn't forgotten. The debt he owed had weighed heavy on his mind over the past weeks. But since she'd presented her ludicrous proposal, he'd hoped like hell she wouldn't remember. He had every intention of returning the favor. Somehow. Someway. If he did not, he would suffer for all eternity, for his soul would not be permitted to cross over to the other side. However, he refused to believe that the gift would take the form of a wedding band. It wouldn't if there was any chance he could avoid it.

"Life Gift," he corrected her. "I owe you a Life Gift." He pulled his hands free from his pockets and lifted them, palms up. "Before you left me there on the road, you asked me to pray for your sister. I did that."

"But your prayer didn't keep Amy alive, now did it?"

They stared at each other in silence. Finally, he said, "You can't expect me to marry you."

"Why?" True concern creased her forehead. "Do your beliefs dictate against such a union? Marrying out of need rather than love?"

"No." He shook his head. Were he not an honorable man, he'd lie his way out of this. "But you have to agree, you're asking an awful lot of me here. Even if I would consider it, the Elders aren't going to be fooled, Jenna. They won't trust a marriage that's coming at them out of the blue. They'd be suspicious. Surely, they'd require that you live here. On the rez. With me. Your husband."

"I'm prepared to do that," she told him. Her face was still damp, but hope shone in her still-moist eyes and eagerness brightened her tone. "A couple of months should do it, don't you think? Surely not more than three."

"But I don't even know you." He planted his hands on his hips, baffled by the fact that she was truly serious about this outrageous idea.

"Within three months," she continued in a rush, "I'm certain I can win them over. I can prove to the Elders that I'm worthy to raise Lily. They'll see me everywhere with her. I'll attend all of the community functions. I'll even participate. You have gatherings and special celebrations, right? I read about them in the paper all the time." She didn't wait for an answer. "And anytime we're away from the ranch, I'll play the part of a loving and devoted wife so no one will ever know of our marriage pact. I promise you that the truth will never come out. I'll need to learn all I can about your culture if I'm to teach Lily. I can't start too soon with something so important, right? The Council will love my attitude on that subject, don't you—"

"Jenna! Stop!"

She went quiet.

"I can't do this." He let the words sink in, and then he firmly repeated, "I can't."

He braced himself for more tears, but what he hadn't prepared himself for was the tenacity that firmed her jaw.

"So your life isn't worth three measly months of your time?"

Accusation made her question uncomfortably sharp. Without breaking eye contact with him, she sniffed and reached up to rub the tip of her nose with the back of her hand.

Shame fell on his shoulders like a load of cinder blocks. He tried to shrug the feeling off, but it only grew heavier. He frowned.

He would not allow her to humiliate him into doing something—

"Do you owe me, Gage Dalton? The day of the storm, you made this Life Gift sound like a very serious thing."

She had no idea just how serious.

Chagrin shot through him like white-hot lightning, and she clearly sensed it. He knew she could tell what her allegations were doing to him. And it only made her doggedness all the stronger.

She folded her arms across her chest. "So…are you going to pay your debt, or aren't you?"

Jenna Butler had him backed into a corner, and there wasn't a damned thing he could do about it.

"And you have proof that this marriage is actually going to take place?"

Disapproval tightened the shaman's wrinkled face. Of all the Elders sitting at the long oak table, Chee'pai had presented Jenna with the most vehement resistance. A contrary man, he'd been adamant from day one that Lily not leave the reservation.

"Of course," Jenna told him. Nerves writhed in her stomach, turned her knees jelly-weak, but she made every effort to keep her hand from trembling when she offered the marriage license to him. He took it from her. Although he hadn't ever been blatantly disrespectful, Jenna never failed to feel the mighty weight of his condemnation during the many Council meetings she'd attended. The man was simply and clearly opposed to her gaining custody of Lily.

He didn't bother to look at the legal document but demanded. "Why did you not tell us of your plans to marry before today?"

Jenna squared her shoulders. "You didn't ask."

Chee'pai scowled at what he obviously perceived as impertinence.

"I have answered all your questions," she reminded him. She let her gaze trail down the row of men and women. "I have held nothing back. Not one of you can say differently. How could I have answered questions that haven't been asked?"

No one offered an argument.

"And this man is Indian?" another council member asked.

"He is Delaware," Jenna said. "He lives on Broken Bow. And Lily and I will live here, too…with him. We'll be married at the courthouse in Forsyth just as soon as the blood test results are in."

Montana's required test for rubella was all that stood between Jenna and Lily.

"It shouldn't take long. The lab tech promised to rush things for me." She clamped her lips shut. She was talking too fast, submitting too much information.

Gage had offered to come with her to this meeting,

but Jenna had felt the need to face the group alone, to see this fight to the end on her own.

Chee'pai almost shoved her license at the Elder sitting to his left, a man who actually scrutinized the paper. Something in the document made the man grow still, but Jenna didn't have time to wonder what it might be before Chee'pai addressed the group.

"For me," the shaman announced, "this changes nothing."

Disappointment assailed her. She must keep a positive attitude. This man was one voice among eight. Surely, someone in the group would see reason. If no one did, she was going to have to think fast.

Gage had warned her against lying to the Elders. To do so would forever jeopardize her integrity in the eyes of the Council. Jenna had planned to speak nothing but the truth; however, desperation often made people do things they wouldn't normally do, say things they wouldn't normally say, act in ways that were alien. Hopefully, the Elders wouldn't push her to those extremes.

That was one of the reasons she'd come alone. If she were forced to say or do anything reckless, she didn't want Gage to be tainted by her wayward behavior.

The marriage license continued down the row of solemn-faced Council members.

"I have a question."

The woman who spoke had vivid green eyes. Her long gray hair was parted in the middle and trailed over her shoulders in two thick braids. Her bony shoulders were rounded by the years.

"I mean no disrespect," the woman continued, "but

I'd like to know when you met your fiancé. How long have you known each other?"

Anxiety flared like hungry flames, threatening to consume Jenna. Although there hadn't been any direct accusation in the questions they'd asked, this was as close as any of them had come to suggesting she might be up to something not quite legitimate. Obviously, they'd be suspicious of the marriage. It would be silly for Jenna to think otherwise. However, before this moment, none of them had implied that she might be scheming in order to gain custody of Lily. She'd expected Chee'pai would have been the one who might make blatant charges, but it seemed that doubt had others willing to question her, as well.

Garnering control of her voice, Jenna said, "I met him before this…situation began. Before my sister died."

It was not a lie. Jenna voiced the words with a clear conscience.

The woman nodded and said nothing more.

Hoo'ma sat at the very end of the table, and she had just finished studying Jenna's license. The old woman's nut-brown eyes flashed with astonishment, and Jenna grew curious. What on earth was the woman thinking? Why had many of the Elders reacted to the license with what looked to be surprise?

Hoo'ma radiated calmness, even in her silence.

Over the weeks of this ordeal, Jenna had discovered that Hoo'ma was well respected by the other Council members. It was apparent that she was the oldest member of the Council, and Jenna had inadvertently learned that her name meant *grandmother* in the language of this tribe. She didn't speak often, but when she did, everyone paid close attention.

Hoo'ma leaned her frail body forward, and all eyes turned to her.

"I see that you are to marry Gage Dalton," she said.

Jenna went still. Something had sparked in the wizened woman's tone when she uttered Gage's name. It was as if she wanted the others to pay attention, to take special note. The Elders who hadn't had a chance to see the certificate for themselves did just that; the ones who had read it nodded in silent agreement. But what exactly were they acknowledging? Their reaction was puzzling.

"Gage plans to take this woman as his wife?" Incredulity sharpened Chee'pai's question.

Hoo'ma ignored him. Lacing her knobby fingers together, she rested her hands on the tabletop and addressed Jenna. "Marriage is a sacred union, my child. The ties that bind men and women may vary. Some are brought together by love. Others by necessity. Even others by—" one of her shoulders lifted a fraction "—who knows what reasons? But the bonds between a husband and wife are the threads that hold together the very universe, and they could not—and would not— happen if the Great One opposed."

Several aged gazes slid from Hoo'ma's. The woman's unspoken chastisement thickened the air. Evidently, Hoo'ma thought the doubtful questions about this impending marriage were inappropriate.

"I would like to take this opportunity to congratulate you," she continued to address Jenna. "On behalf of the Council, I wish you and Gage every happiness." She swiveled her head to take in her fellow Council members. "Now, I think the time has come to allow Lily to go to her rightful home."

"Ma'ta!" Chee'pai stood.

The opposition in the man's tone couldn't be missed, and Jenna knew the man said no in his native tongue.

"Our tribe is dwindling by the moment!" The shaman's face was fury-red. "We send our children off to colleges and they do not return. Our young adults leave Broken Bow for jobs in the city. If we allow this to continue, our clan will be no more!"

Unruffled by Chee'pai's outburst, Hoo'ma looked past the shaman and directed her attention to the others at the table.

"Jenna has complied with our every demand with patience." The woman's wrinkled cheeks bore the hint of a smile as she murmured, "For the most part." She slid her folded hands into her lap. "She has promised to respect Lily's Delaware heritage. It is our tradition to give our children roots." She squared herself to Chee'pai as she added, "It is also our tradition to give them wings. If the roots are deep enough, they will not forget from where they come."

The shaman seethed, but he did not speak.

"This marriage is a good thing," Hoo'ma said. "As soon as Jenna and Gage are wed, they should have Lily. They should become a family. I can feel healing and enlightenment approaching. For all concerned. I am surprised, Chee'pai, that you haven't felt it, too." After a pause that obviously called for reflection, she pronounced, "Let us vote."

Chapter Three

"Are you upset about the civil service?" Jenna had finally garnered enough courage to ask the question that had been rolling in her mind since they'd left the courthouse. She glanced at Gage tentatively.

"Why would I be upset?" His attention never wavered from the road ahead as he drove his pickup on I-94 toward Broken Bow. "Other than the fact that I hadn't planned on repaying a Life Gift with wedding vows."

She ignored his murmured aside. She couldn't regret having pledged herself to Gage in front of a Rosebud County clerk of the court. The marriage certificate in her possession was mandatory in gaining custody of Lily. To Jenna, it hadn't mattered that the ceremony was short and quite dispassionate. Even with the requested rush on the tests, the wait for results had meant another excruciating week without Lily. The truth be known, Jenna was relieved to have the formalities over so quickly.

She had her doubts about Gage.

"Well," she began, "my guess is that you're, um, a very spiritual person. I thought that you might have felt peculiar about going to the courthouse to get married as opposed to…" She faltered for a moment. "Well, as opposed to having a religious ceremony."

"And you came to those conclusions merely because I'm Indian?"

Accusation edged the question, and Jenna felt suddenly self-conscious. She hadn't meant to offend him.

Before she could respond, he said, "You shouldn't form opinions about Native Americans based solely on stereotypes."

Now she felt insulted herself. "I was doing no such thing."

The raised brows on his chiseled profile were clear evidence that he was unconvinced.

"I wasn't," she insisted, shifting on the seat.

"So why would you think I'd be upset that we married at the courthouse?" he pressed.

She lifted one shoulder a fraction. "Because of the things you said the day we met. You used a name… Kitan To-wet—" her tongue tripped over the foreign word "—I think it was. You spoke as if this was some great force or entity. Like fate. Or God." Heat flushed her cheeks when she realized how this must sound to him, as if she had him figured out because of the things he'd said that day. "You said Kitan To-wet had plans for you, and that I'd messed up those plans."

"Kit-tan-it-to'wet," he corrected. "It's Algonquian for Great Spirit. It's our name for God."

She nodded, relieved that, although she hadn't pronounced the name perfectly, she hadn't completely mangled it beyond recognition.

"And you seemed very passionate," she continued, "about repaying the debt you felt you owed me. All that led me to believe you were—" again she shrugged "—a spiritual man."

He was silent as they left the interstate, the exit ramp winding around to a bridge that crossed Yellowstone River.

"I owe you an apology." His gaze connected with hers for a fraction of a second. "In my business, I sometimes come into contact with…people. People who tend to put me in some sort of box, or expect me to fit some sort of mold. Because I'm Delaware. Because I'm Indian."

"White people," she supplied.

His silence was proof that she'd presumed correctly.

"Tell you what," she said. "I promise not to stereotype you because you're Delaware if you promise not to stereotype me because I'm white."

The lightness in her tone succeeded in dissolving the tension in him. His shoulders relaxed, and when he looked at her, he was actually smiling. It was the first time she'd seen him smile, and the curling at the corners of his wide mouth made his already striking features downright mesmerizing. Her pulse kicked into high gear and the interior of the truck's cab became unbearably hot.

"You've got a deal," he told her softly.

The smile she offered was weak, at best. For the first time since approaching him for help, she felt that they'd connected.

And the feeling was darned disconcerting.

Jenna swallowed, broke eye contact and gazed out over the Montana grassland. Her new husband could easily become a distraction. And a distraction was one thing she didn't need. She was going to have her hands full caring for Lily and keeping up with her business. She'd worked hard to build her reputation, and she didn't want to lose it. She'd been dubbed "the Webmaster whiz" by the companies who contracted her to build and maintain their Web sites. And as Jenna figured it, with Lily still a baby, she would only be able to work when her niece napped in the afternoon or slumbered through the night. It wasn't going to be easy, but it wasn't any more difficult than what any other new mother experienced juggling a job and a child.

That was how she thought of herself.

Gage steered the pickup onto Reservation Road.

"You want to pick up your niece now?"

She hadn't expected the offer. "Yes. If that's okay with you, I mean. If you have to get back to the ranch to tend to the horses, I can come back for her. I don't want to put you out."

"If it wasn't okay with me, I wouldn't have suggested it."

"Oh." Excitement tickled the pit of her belly. "Okay, then. Yes. That would be wonderful."

No fanfare marked the entrance to Broken Bow Reservation. Just a worn sign with black block letters and a directional arrow. The reservation itself was quite basic. The main road wove through a small village that wasn't even big enough to be called a town, really. There was a general store, a sheriff's office, a post office, a restaurant called Hannah's Home-Style Diner, a community center that doubled as an information office for the odd tourist who happened by for a visit and the Council building that Jenna had become so familiar with over the past couple of months. Small, neat homes lined both sides of the street. Anyone else would describe the place as plain, but at this moment she thought it was the most beautiful place on Earth. She was going to see Lily, and she would be taking the baby home with her at last.

Well, not home, exactly, but it was close enough for now.

Joy made her feel featherlight. She was so happy, she could barely contain the bubbly emotion. She pressed her fingertips against her lips, fearing she might break out in sudden laughter.

She'd done it. She'd bested the Elders. She'd won her battle for custody of her sister's baby girl. Surely, things would sail smoothly for her and Lily from here on out.

Gage pulled up to the curb in front of Arlene Johnson's house. In her mid-fifties, Arlene was a widow whose one grown daughter, Hannah, owned the restaurant down the street. Arlene loved children and ran a daycare center in her home. Jenna had come to know Arlene well over these past weeks of battling with the Council of Elders, and the two of them had become friends. Although the woman had sympathized with Jenna's plight from day one, she'd also been staunch in her adamancy that the Council's dictates be followed to the letter.

Jenna opened the door of the truck even before the vehicle came to a complete halt. "I'll be right back," she called over her shoulder. She stopped suddenly, and turned back. "Unless you want to come in."

"I'll wait."

Was his grip on the steering wheel tighter than necessary? Jenna let the question go unexplored as the thrill of the moment swept her up once again.

"I'll hurry," she said, and then jogged up the cement walkway toward Arlene's house.

Her friend must have been watching for her because the door opened when Jenna stepped onto the porch.

Arlene cradled a sleeping Lily in her arms. "Good morning. So everything's official?"

"Sure is." Jenna stepped into the neat living room, her eyes locking onto her niece. "Can I hold her?" she asked, grinning.

The transfer went so smoothly that the baby didn't even stir.

Jenna kissed Lily's forehead tenderly.

"Congratulations," Arlene told her.

"Thanks," Jenna breathed. "I've been dreaming about this day for a long time. I was beginning to think I'd never get custody of Lily."

Arlene was quiet for a moment. Then she said, "I'm happy about that, too. But I was congratulating you on your marriage."

"Oh. Of course. Thank you." Jenna occupied herself with smoothing out Lily's light cotton receiving blanket.

"Jenna." Arlene's tone was soft. "You did get married for the right reason, didn't you?"

She lifted her gaze to her friend's and never wavered as she proclaimed, "I got married for the best possible reason."

Although the woman nodded, Jenna could tell she remained speculative.

"I'd love to stay and chat," Jenna said, "but Gage is waiting in the truck and we need to get home and get settled."

"I've got Lily's things packed and ready to go. And the car seat is right here, too. I'll help you carry everything out."

"Thanks."

As the women approached the truck, Gage got out, rounded the truck and took Lily's small suitcase from Arlene. Jenna noticed that Gage's greeting to Arlene wasn't the friendliest, but it was clear he knew the woman. He moved to the back end of the vehicle to stow the case.

"Want me to secure the car seat?" Arlene asked.

"I'll do it." Jenna handed Lily back to Arlene. "I need to figure out how it works sooner or later."

Gage's pickup had a small bench seat behind the front seat. Jenna figured this would be a safer place for Lily. She struggled with the car seat's straps and buckles for several frustrating minutes and then turned to Arlene.

"The belt won't snap."

"Let me try." Arlene handed the baby over.

Jenna smiled. "Don't you just love baby juggling?"

Arlene chuckled. "It's the best kind of juggling there is."

While Arlene bent over the car seat, Jenna glanced toward the back of the truck at Gage. He looked tense, staring off at the horizon.

"Got it," Arlene pronounced. She backed her way out of the truck's cab and turned to Jenna. "It'll just take a little practice. Car seats fit in each vehicle differently. You'll get the hang of it quickly, I'm sure."

Jenna tucked the sleeping Lily in the seat and fastened the belt across her little chest with a click. Then she gave Arlene a big hug. "Thanks for everything. Taking care of Lily. The endless cups of tea. And all the listening you did. You're a wonderful friend."

"So are you. Lily's lucky to have someone in the world who loves her so much."

They shared a warm smile.

Finally, Jenna called out to Gage, "Ready."

"If you ever need a sitter," Arlene said, "don't hesitate to call me."

"I won't." Jenna got into the truck. "Lily and I will come for a visit soon," she promised from the open window.

Arlene nodded and waved as Gage drove away.

Immediately, Jenna worried if the breeze was too much for the baby, and she pressed the switch to close the window.

"You okay?" she asked Gage.

"I'm fine."

"You don't seem fine. You seem uptight. Really uptight. Do you know Arlene?"

"Everyone knows Arlene Johnson. I attended school with her daughter, Hannah."

Lily stirred behind them, and Jenna twisted around to check on her. The baby sighed in her sleep.

"Do you not like Arlene or something? Has she done something to you?" Jenna pressed, settling herself in the seat once again.

"I like her fine." His tone sounded clipped. "Arlene has nothing to do with this."

"So there *is* something wrong?"

For a moment, all Jenna heard was the whine of tires on asphalt and she thought he meant to simply ignore her question. He was well within his rights to do so. She never should have pursued the subject this far.

Finally, Gage said, "There is nothing wrong, Jenna." His black eyes zeroed in on her. "Let it go."

The remainder of the ride was made in silence.

Gage's ranch house was larger than Jenna remembered. A gable roof cut through the center of it, wings extending to both the east and west sides. Jenna surmised that the windowed wall that was a focal point from outside must be the main living area. Beautiful in its rustic simplicity, the ranch blended well with the lush and sweeping Montana landscape.

Once Gage cut the engine, Jenna got out of the truck and immediately took Lily from the car seat. The baby opened sleepy eyes and yawned.

"Are you awake?" Jenna said softly.

Lily offered a sleepy grin, and Jenna's heart swelled with warmth.

"You're such a good girl."

"Are you coming?" Gage called from the porch. "I'll give you a quick tour before I head out to the stable."

Jenna was surprised to see that he'd already plucked Lily's diaper bag and suitcase from the back of the truck and was unlocking the front door. She hitched Lily onto her hip and hurried around the truck.

As she'd guessed, the front door opened into a large living area. Both the front and the back of the room featured glass walls that revealed spectacular north and south views of the ranch. One end was obviously used as a media center, complete with stereo and television. At the other end were plenty of book-filled shelves and several comfy chairs. A large stone fireplace in the center of the room separated the areas. Jenna could easily imagine snuggling near a blazing fire while she read a cozy mystery during one of those awesome Montana snowstorms. But she'd never experience that kind of indulgence because she didn't expect to live in Gage's home that long. If her plans unfolded properly, she and Lily would be in her apartment in Rock Springs by fall.

"Make yourself at home while you're here," he said. "I have cable TV, and quite a few DVDs to choose from in the cabinet there. And lots of CDs, as well. I guess you can see I like to read. You're welcome to entertain yourself."

Although his small speech was convivial, the underlying tightness in his tone couldn't be missed.

"Thanks," Jenna murmured. "But between taking care of Lily and keeping up with my work, I doubt I'll have time for much entertainment."

"You're planning to work?"

"Of course. I can't let my business falter."

Lily grabbed a fistful of Jenna's hair and tried to stuff it into her mouth. Jenna said, "Don't, honey. Here. This is better." She offered the baby the pacifier that was clipped to her pink bib.

"Your business?" Gage asked. "I don't understand. Who'll watch your niece?"

"I will. I've always worked from home. That's why it was so easy for me to relocate to Broken Bow. I can work from any location." She shifted Lily to her left hip. "I build and maintain Web sites. All I need is a place to set up my computer, and access to the Internet. You said you have cable. That's great. I'll have to call the company and sign up for high-speed Internet service. I'll pay, of course. It's a business expense."

Lily patted Jenna's cheek, and Jenna smiled into her niece's face. When she looked at Gage again, he seemed edgy and she feared she was keeping him from his work.

He gestured toward the east wing. "Kitchen and dining rooms are down that way. Bedrooms are this way."

Jenna followed him down the hallway that ran the length of the west wing. There were four doors, two on each side.

They passed what she guessed was the master bedroom. The door was open and she glimpsed a neatly made king-size bed.

The door was closed to the room directly across from the master bedroom, and Gage passed it without comment.

"Here we are," he said, setting the diaper bag and

suitcase on the bed in one of the remaining two rooms. "I hope it's not a problem for you and your niece to share."

"It's no problem. The bed's plenty big. We can make it work." She looked at the baby. "It'll be an adventure, right, Lily?"

The bedroom was ample for her needs. Tastefully decorated in summery shades of yellow, it housed a queen-size bed, a dresser and a small desk. The south-facing window offered sunny exposure.

"This is perfect," she told Gage. She grinned at Lily again. "It's perfect for us, isn't it, sweet stuff?"

Obviously enjoying her aunt's attention, the baby garbled a nonsensical reply.

"See?" Jenna grinned at Gage. "Lily thinks so, too."

The tension emanating from him was unmistakable now, and Jenna suddenly felt guilty.

"I'm sorry I kept you so long. I'm sure you've got work to do. I assume the bathroom is across the hall." She bent and set Lily down on the carpet.

Visibly relieved that she'd given him leave, he made a beeline for the door, but paused at the threshold to ask, "Can I bring your things in for you?"

When she'd arrived from Rock Springs this morning, she'd been running late and hadn't had time to unpack her computer and her belongings from the car. Gage had been waiting for her on the front porch and they had gotten directly into his truck and headed for their appointment at the courthouse in Forsyth.

"Thanks, but don't bother." Jenna pulled some soft toys from the diaper bag and offered them to Lily.

"There's no rush. I'll grab what I need later, then un-pack the car as soon as I can find some free time. I got myself caught up on work so I could have a few days to focus on Lily."

He nodded. "I'll be out at the stable if you need me." Then he disappeared from view.

She looked around, frowning at the thought of set-ting up her computer in here. She'd have to work while Lily was sleeping and she wouldn't want to disturb her niece. She hurried to the bedroom door.

"Gage."

He turned to face her at the end of the hallway.

"What's in there?" she asked, pointing to the closed door across from the master bedroom. "I was hoping it might be a room where I could work. You know, so I wouldn't disturb Lily if she's sleeping."

His wide mouth flattened. "Off-limits," was all he said before turning on his heel and stalking away.

She backed into her bedroom unable to decide if she should feel merely surprised by the man's terse response or insulted by it.

"What do you think, sweet stuff?" she asked Lily in a singsong voice. She picked up the baby, then laid her down on the bed for a diaper change. "Is Gage a big, ol' meany-beany?" She placed her index finger on the tip of her niece's nose and gave it a wiggle. Lily giggled. "Or is that closed door none of Auntie Jenna's business?"

The baby gurgled and munched on the rubber nipple of the pacifier.

"Ah, so you agree that it's none of my business, huh?" Jenna pulled loose the tape tabs of the damp disposable diaper and tugged it from underneath Lily's chubby bottom. "I think you may be right."

With her hand firmly on Lily's bare belly, Jenna searched the diaper bag and found that Arlene had stuffed it full of supplies—diapers, rash cream, a couple cans of formula, a box of baby cereal and several jars of fruit. Jenna made a mental note to thank her friend for her thoughtfulness.

As she cleaned Lily's bottom with a moist towelette, she couldn't help but think about the off-limits room.

The ranch he was running was a business. The room across the hall was probably his office. Why hadn't she thought of that before?

He could have just told her. He needn't have been so short.

But he'd been antsy to get to work. And she'd kept him from the stable all morning to endure the civil service.

Jenna thought about the ceremony that had made the two of them husband and wife. The room, the words, even the clerk had been austere. It certainly hadn't been the wedding of her dreams. Not by any stretch of the imagination. However, no one would ever hear a peep of complaint out of her because the vows she'd spoken to become Mrs. Gage Dalton made it possible for her to attain the most important prize of all.

Lily.

She could afford to forgive Gage his curtness because of all he'd made possible for her.

Putting the spartan civil ceremony and the door across the hall completely out of her mind, Jenna spent a good hour playing with the baby. She sang silly, made-up songs, played patty-cake and peekaboo, and laughed at each and every one of the animated faces that Lily made. Her sister's daughter was a happy child, and, from what she'd learned researching child development on the Internet, Lily seemed to be right on track with her physical progress.

At just over six months, Lily was sitting on her own, could roll over in both directions, reached for objects she wanted, jabbered in response to verbal stimulus, and, when lying flat on her tummy, she was attempting to lift herself onto her hands and knees. She would be crawling soon.

Suddenly, Jenna grew solemn. It was such a shame that Amy and David weren't here to witness their daughter's achievements. But she shook herself out of her melancholy mood quickly.

"Today's not a day for sadness," Jenna said aloud. "Today's a day for celebration. You and I are going to be together forever and ever, aren't we, sweet stuff?" She kissed her niece on the forehead.

Surprisingly, Lily didn't seem to like the kiss. In fact, Jenna noticed that the baby was becoming a tad crabby. Glancing at her watch, Jenna asked, "Are you hungry, sweet stuff?"

She picked Lily up. On their way toward the kitchen, Jenna saw her things lined up neatly on the floor by the front door. Gage had carried them in for her.

He certainly was a mysterious man. Blunt and almost unfriendly one moment, and then unexpectedly thoughtful the next.

While Lily busied herself on the floor with some pot lids, Jenna set about stirring up some baby cereal using the package directions. Next, she opened a small jar of processed peaches. But once she began attempting to feed Lily lunch, Jenna quickly realized she was going to have to buy a high chair. By the time Lily was fed, both she and the baby were splattered with bits of cereal and strained peaches. She'd been so busy fighting to win custody, she hadn't given a thought to high chairs, cribs, strollers and the like.

Once she had given Lily a bath and changed her clothes, it was clear the grumpy child was in need of an afternoon nap. Forty minutes later, though, Jenna was at her wit's end. Lily had cried and cried. Jenna had paced the floor, cradling her niece, until the baby finally fell asleep, exhausted. Carefully, Jenna laid her down in the very center of the big bed and hemmed her in on all sides with pillows so she couldn't roll off the mattress.

Heaving a huge sigh, Jenna thought about sitting down for a few minutes to rest. But she knew that would be a mistake. Lily wouldn't nap for long, and Jenna had things to do.

Her grumbling stomach sent her back to the kitchen. While making herself a sandwich, she made one for Gage, too, so it would be waiting for him when he returned from the stable. She was tucking it into the refrigerator when he came through the back door.

"I made a sandwich for you," she told him by way of greeting, setting the food on the table.

He nodded and silently moved around her to the sink. He turned on the faucet and squirted liquid soap into his palm from the pump dispenser nearby.

"Call it a payback." She smiled, and he just looked at her. "For carrying in my stuff. Thanks for doing that."

His head bobbed again, a lock of his black hair falling over his shoulder. Jenna wondered if it would feel silky between her fingers, then she quickly snuffed out the errant thought.

The silence in the kitchen seemed to hum. Jenna had no desire to spend the next three months feeling so awkward.

"Listen, Gage—" she picked up the sandwich she'd made herself and went to the table to sit down "—I'm sorry I kept you from your work this morning. I'm sorry if I caused you to fall behind in—"

"I'm not behind."

She knew she was already feeling frustrated from her experience trying to get Lily to sleep. The fact that he interrupted her with such a terse response was as irritating as sitting on a purposefully placed tack on the seat of her chair.

"Well, if you're not anxious about the horses," she blustered, "if you're not behind in your chores, then why the heck are you so grouchy? You've been short since we picked up Lily. If you don't like having two women under your roof, then I'm sorry, but it won't be long before—"

"I like women just fine."

Again with the interruption. Again with the clipped reply. What was the man's problem?

And then she realized what it was. She'd just spelled it out herself. His demeanor had turned stiff the moment they stopped at Arlene's for Lily. At first, Jenna had thought he had something against Arlene. Then she'd thought he was just anxious to get out to the stable. But now she realized that he hadn't made even one attempt to interact with Lily, hadn't touched her, hadn't talked to her, hadn't smiled at her, nothing.

"You don't like children." Incredulity coated her tone, but Jenna didn't care. How on earth could *anyone* not love a baby girl as cute and cuddly as Lily?

A muscle in his jaw twitched. "What I'm going through is personal. I agreed to marry you so you could get custody of your niece. I didn't agree to open up my personal life."

Jenna slid the sandwich several inches away from her. She'd lost her appetite. "You might not want to talk about this, but I think it's pretty important. Lily's only a baby, yes. But I'm sure she's going to sense your feelings toward her. And you're not going to make her feel safe. You stopped so we could pick Lily up, yes, but other than that you haven't acknowledged her at all."

"Look around, Jenna. There's more work out there than one man can do. This is a horse ranch, not some cutesy baby ranch. I didn't sign on to be that child's daddy."

Shock made her jaw go slack for an instant. "I never asked that of you."

"Good. Because it isn't going to happen."

Feeling strangely rejected and not understanding why, Jenna just sat there. Finally, she calmly said, "Gage, I don't know what your problem is, but I'm not going to allow you to treat Lily badly."

"Then the thing you need to do—" he snatched up the sandwich she'd made him and stalked to the back door "—is keep her away from me." The door slammed in his wake.

Chapter Four

Lily slapped her hand on the surface of the water, the resulting splash eliciting bubbly laughter from her. The baby enjoyed her bath time, no doubt about it. She could be completely out of sorts, but the moment Jenna turned on the faucet and began undressing her, Lily would grin and coo and kick her legs excitedly.

The past four days had been a crash course in parenting for Jenna. She'd thought that her thorough Internet research prior to gaining custody of Lily had prepared for the task of raising her sister's baby. But what she'd learned was that nothing could prepare one for the frequently satisfying, occasionally frightening, oftentimes frustrating and chronically exhausting job called motherhood.

Bedtime was the worst. In fact, Jenna had come to

dread it. Lily seemed to struggle against her body's need for sleep. She was sure the baby wanted her mother, and she did all she could to soothe and comfort Lily. But her niece seemed inconsolable. After what seemed like hours, Lily would finally drop off into a deep slumber only to jerk awake after ninety minutes or so, and the whole jarring routine would begin again. Jenna had gotten to the point that she was a nervous wreck, lying awake in the dark just waiting for the baby to start crying.

She'd tried every suggestion she could find on the Internet baby sites, and she'd called Arlene for advice, too. She rocked, she sang, she walked the floors. Most nights, she ended up moving to the other side of the house, pacing through the kitchen and dining rooms with Lily so as not to disturb Gage. Nothing seemed to help. And after four nights with little sleep, Jenna was truly suffering. The dull ache at the base of her skull refused to go away. Her eyes were bleary, and her temper was short.

Jenna let Lily play in the tub until the tiny pads of her fingers were wrinkled and the water turned tepid.

"Okay, sweet stuff." Her words came out on a weary sigh as she lifted Lily from the water. "Time for nighty-night."

The large terry towel made short work of drying the baby after which Jenna put a diaper on Lily, followed by a pair of pajamas made of whisper-soft jersey. She crossed the hall to their bedroom and sat in the chair, cuddling Lily in her lap, then opened a picture book just as she had every night since moving into Gage's home.

Every article she'd read recommended a strict nighttime routine. Even Arlene had said that following a schedule was important. Hopefully, Lily would soon get used to falling asleep in her new surroundings.

However, just as Jenna had feared, it didn't take long before Lily was rubbing her eyes, squirming and whimpering. And thirty minutes later, Jenna felt like crying herself.

"Okay, okay," she whispered in a soothing voice. "Let's take a walk." Jenna stood, turned Lily so the baby's head rested on her shoulder, and picked up a light receiving blanket on the way out of the bedroom.

Jenna hummed as she made her way down the hall and into the living room, smoothing her flattened palm against the baby's back. Fatigue had her feeling impatient and she hoped Lily didn't sense that.

The sound of the back door opening and closing told her that Gage had come in from the stable. After he'd so bluntly told her that he wasn't interested in dealing with Lily, Jenna had decided it would be best to avoid him as much as possible. As it turned out, doing so hadn't been a problem. He rose early and stayed out with the horses most of the day, returning to the house only to grab a quick meal or make a phone call or two. Jenna had no idea what he did out there in the stable and other outbuildings. She'd been too busy with Lily, trying to unpack and get settled to give it much thought.

She'd borrowed a high chair from Arlene, but realized that the other big-ticket items she needed required a trip into Forsyth. However, transporting a stroller and a crib and mattress would require the use of Gage's pickup. And since they weren't exactly speaking, she hadn't made it to town.

Gage hadn't even approached her to complain that Lily was disturbing his sleep, and Jenna couldn't imagine that the baby's crying *hadn't* been keeping him awake. The first couple of days, she'd worried about it. But as the seemingly endless days and sleepless nights wore on, she just didn't have the energy to feel too concerned about Gage.

Jenna looked at the whimpering baby and regretted her silent complaints. The good far outweighed the bad. Lily filled her days with many moments of sheer delight, but a body simply couldn't go for days without rest.

Gage nodded at her in greeting when he entered the living room, his mouth a firm, straight line.

"I made dinner," she told him over Lily's cries. "It's not much. I opened a tin of soup and made sandwiches. The soup just needs reheating, and your sandwich is in the fridge. I'd offer to—"

"Don't give it another thought," he said.

He'd told her early on she didn't have to cook for him, but it was just as easy to prepare a meal for two as it was for one.

"I'm going to get a quick shower," he told her.

As Jenna paced back toward the bedroom with the baby, she heard the water running in Gage's master bath. She sat down in the chair and rocked Lily, hoping she could get the baby to sleep before he finished.

Although he wasn't outright hostile, he was quite cool. Her time in his home—in their short-lived marriage— didn't have to be like this. His unwillingness to make the best of the few months she'd asked for had proved without too much doubt that he had a wintry personality.

Maybe he had perfectly good reasons for his behavior, but right now Jenna was simply too drained to ponder them.

Nearly twenty minutes later, the baby's sobs persisted in tearing at her heart and jarring her nerves. The dull ache in her head had transformed into a pounding pain. She'd gone back to pacing and returned to the living room.

"Lily," she murmured as calmly as she could, "please stop crying. Relax. *Please,* sweet stuff."

"Jenna."

She whirled at the sound of Gage's voice, unaware that he'd come into the living room.

His long hair was damp. He sometimes secured it with an elastic band at the back of his neck, but now it hung loose about his shoulders. The fabric of the fresh gray cotton T-shirt he wore pulled taut across his broad chest, and a pair of black jeans hugged his thighs. His feet were bare and nicely shaped. She realized her gaze had lingered on them several seconds too long.

She dragged her gaze back to his face. And although she was tired to the marrow of her bones, she couldn't stop the wayward thought running through her mind…the man's physique was impressive.

Blinking several times, she inhaled deeply.

"I'm sorry if she's disturbing you," she said. "I'm sure she'll be asleep soon. She simply can't hold out much longer."

She fully expected him to march off to the kitchen,

but he took her completely by surprise when he came closer. The heated soapy scent of him swirled around her.

"May I?"

Jenna wasn't sure what he was asking, but then he reached out his hands. Stunned, she searched his gaze.

"Let me have a go at this," he said softly.

Jenna handed over the baby to Gage. It was amazing that someone so big and formidable could be so gentle.

"Hey, Lily," he greeted. He didn't smile, but his tone was affable.

Jenna couldn't say the exact moment the baby stopped crying. She didn't know if it had been upon Gage's approach, or at the sound of his voice, or when he'd actually scooped her in his arms. Jenna had been too focused on Gage to be conscious of it. All she did know was that the silence was truly blissful.

Lily stared into Gage's face as if she were entranced.

"Can I have that?" he asked, pointing to the receiving blanket that was draped over her shoulder.

"Sure."

Their fingers brushed when she handed it over, his work-roughened skin warm against her own.

He moved to the couch, spread the blanket on the cushion as best he could with one hand and then placed Lily on it.

"Little ones like to be bundled up," he said. He wrapped the baby in a neat little package, tucking the blanket around her. "It reminds them of the security they felt in their mother's womb."

Jenna hadn't read that tidbit of advice on any of the Web sites she'd visited. All she could do was gawk as he picked up the now quiet baby and cradled her in the crook of his right arm.

"Come," he said to Jenna. "Sit down. You look like…well, like you could use a break."

Jenna was too darned tired to even smile at his remark. "You're being kind, I'm sure. I look like a bad train wreck."

"I wouldn't say that."

She paused before sitting down, some unexpected tone in his voice impelling her to take a moment to study his handsome face. But she wasn't able to discern if some hidden meaning lurked behind what he'd said, or if he was merely being polite.

Sighing, Jenna took a seat and reclined against the couch back. "I feel as if I've been rocking her for hours. It hasn't been that long, I know, but…"

Lily let out the cutest coo Jenna had ever heard, and Gage chuckled. Although an unmistakable nervousness edged the sound, his deep, soft laughter resonated through her being.

"I understand what you're saying," he said, his eyes never leaving Lily. "There's something about that cry that breaks your heart. And you have no idea if you're meeting their needs. The fact that they can't clearly communicate what they want with words makes it all the more frustrating."

Ah, Jenna thought, so Lily's crying *had* disturbed his sleep.

Amazed at the baby's reaction to Gage, Jenna said, "Look at how she's staring. It's almost as if you've hypnotized her or something."

He smiled down at the baby and, again, chuckled. And for the second time, Jenna felt the vibration hum through her. She liked the sound. More than she probably should.

"It could be that I've triggered a memory of her father."

"Could be," Jenna agreed. "David had dark eyes, too. And he kept his hair long, like yours."

But her brother-in-law hadn't been nearly as handsome as Gage.

The thought made Jenna's breath catch in her throat. Exhaustion was really taking its toll on her.

"She's so quiet," Jenna said, sliding a few inches closer to him. "Maybe I should go lay her down on the bed. Maybe she'll go to sleep."

"And maybe she'll start crying all over again," he said. "She seems content enough right where she is. Why don't you take the opportunity to lay back and rest your eyes?"

"Oh, no." She shook her head hard enough that a lock of her hair fell over her shoulder. "I couldn't do that."

"Of course you can." Gage gathered the baby in his arm, bent over and curled the fingers of his free hand around her ankle. In one fluid motion, he scooted himself off the cushion and lifted her feet onto it.

Jenna was very aware of the heat of his touch on her leg. Before she even realized what was happening, she was lying prone, her head resting against a throw pillow.

"I really shouldn't, Gage," she murmured. "What if Lily starts crying? She fights sleep as if she were a boxer competing for the world title."

"Tell me about it. She's a champ."

She felt guilty again that her niece had been keeping him up during the night, but the humor in his tone helped her to relax. She stifled a yawn.

"Like I said," he continued, easing himself down onto an adjacent chair, "she seems happy at the moment. Close your eyes and enjoy the peace." He smiled. "However fleeting it turns out to be."

She didn't understand why he was being so nice. The drowsiness closing in on her didn't let her think on it too hard.

He had a nice smile, she thought as her eyes fluttered closed. Smiling was something he should do more often.

"I'll work on that."

The rich timbre of his voice sounded soft and fuzzy, as though he'd whispered the response into a long tunnel. Jenna was sure she must have dreamed it. She didn't think she'd voiced her observation aloud. And then she thought no more as she faded into exhausted oblivion.

Jenna stirred and stretched, then opened her eyes with a soporific sigh. The sound of birdsong was so pleasant to her ears that the corners of her mouth curled. The delicious scent of smoky bacon and coffee wafted in the air, and her stomach grumbled.

It was daylight. The realization made her sit up with a jerk, the thin cotton blanket covering her pooling in her lap. The living room was empty, but she heard activity in the kitchen.

She'd slept through the night. Her mind raced back to the evening before. Gage had come to the rescue. Lily had seemed utterly captivated by him. And then he had suggested she rest her eyes.

Could she have slept through Lily's cries? She had been tired, but could she have zonked out to the point that she hadn't heard her niece during the night?

Shoving the blanket aside, Jenna stood. Absently, she combed her fingers through her hair and headed for the kitchen.

"Morning," Gage greeted. "Coffee?" He lifted the pot, obviously in the act of pouring himself a cup.

"That would be heavenly." She accepted the mug he offered, her gaze scanning the room for her niece. Not wanting him to think she was in a panic, she inhaled the rich vapor, and sipped the steaming liquid. "Mmm. This is good. Thanks." But she couldn't keep her next words from tumbling from her lips. "I'm sorry if you were up with Lily through the night."

"I wasn't. I did leave my door open, though, in case she woke up and you didn't hear her."

Jenna thought it sweet that he'd do such a thing. Especially when he'd been so adamant about not wanting to have anything to do with Lily. It didn't make sense, really. And she had no idea why he was being so nice. But it was sweet, nonetheless.

He drank from his mug, then told her, "I haven't been up long myself."

"But…" Jenna cradled the warm mug between both her hands. "Lily slept through the night?"

Gage nodded. "I think both of you needed a good night's sleep. I know I did."

The grin that cocked his lips was sexy, and suddenly

Jenna felt all flushed. She shifted her weight and studied the rim of her mug.

He set his coffee on the counter. Then he turned off the gas and slid the frying pan onto the back burner. "Let's go check on her."

She followed him through the living room. As they moved into the hallway that led to the bedrooms, he said, "I think part of the problem might be that she needs to sleep alone. It could be that sharing a bed with you was disturbing her sleep."

"You think so? That never entered my head. I wanted to buy her a crib, but I hadn't had a chance to ask you about taking the truck into Forsyth."

For a man who'd seemed so tense around a baby, Gage sure knew a lot about how to handle one. Her curiosity got the better of her. Jenna said, "You were so good with her last night. You gave me that golden nugget of advice about bundling her up. How on earth do you know so much about babies?"

He didn't answer her question. He also didn't continue down the hall to her bedroom, instead turning into the room directly across the hall from his. The one he'd specifically told her was off-limits the day she'd arrived. The one she'd thought was his office.

Jenna looked around her in wonder. It was a nursery. A baby's room beautifully decorated in pale shades of yellow and green, pink and blue. The rocking horse positioned in one corner was painted to look just like the pinto ponies that galloped out in the paddock. A border of teddy bears and alphabet blocks and rattles had been stenciled on the walls at ceiling level. White furniture gave the place an airy feel. The room was clean and dust-free. Well kept. Morning sunlight streamed through the gauzy green curtains hanging at the window.

Glancing into the crib, Jenna saw that Lily snoozed peacefully, her tiny thumb stuck into her mouth.

"Gage?" A dozen questions popped into her head, but every single one of them sounded too intrusive, too personal to voice.

Then she remembered the teenage boy at the service station, the one who had been willing to talk about Gage, the one who had mentioned an accident and how it had changed him. She racked her brain trying to remember what else she'd been told.

In an instant, the puzzle pieces slipped, one at a time, into place. And the picture wasn't pretty. Everything Gage had done last night, everything he'd said about Lily—no, about babies in general, she now realized—suddenly took on new meaning.

"Gage—" she knew a frown marred her forehead "—you were a daddy."

She'd meant to speak in an inquiring manner, but she was so certain of his response that her observation came out sounding like a statement of fact.

He nodded, his chin dipping only once, the strain on his face tightening the muscles in his jaws.

She couldn't stop herself from asking, "Are you divorced, or—"

He shook his head.

The magnitude of the implication was overwhelming. "A widower?"

His head bobbed.

"I'm so sorry," she said. "I—I'm just so sorry. I didn't know. I had heard something about an accident. But I had no idea that you'd lost your wife. And child. Gage, I had no idea you'd lost your family. I honestly had no idea."

She was babbling. She also couldn't help the completely normal human curiosity that was hungry for details, but she didn't dare ask insensitive questions.

"Lily's still sleeping and we don't want to wake her." Gage lifted his hand to point to the door. "Let's go into the kitchen where we can talk."

Minutes later, they had refreshed their mugs of coffee and sat at the kitchen table. The bacon sat forgotten on the stove.

"I should apologize for not offering the use of the nursery before, but—"

"It's all right," she quickly assured him. "It's obviously a very private thing. I can understand why you'd want to keep the room…just so. It belonged to your child. If you'd rather Lily not be in there, I can buy a crib. I *planned* to buy one. I'll set it up in my room. We'll be fine."

Jenna fingered the white paper napkin she'd set her mug on, desperate for something to say. "It just never occurred to me that I might be disturbing Lily's sleep. I mean, the bed is plenty big for both of us. And I put pillows around her, so she'd be safe."

Going on about Lily's sleeping arrangement felt wrong after what he'd just confessed, but she'd said she was sorry and couldn't think of another way to express her regret over his situation.

"Don't beat yourself up about it. How could you know?"

Silence fell. Before the moment could become too awkward, Jenna said, "I'm serious, Gage. I can buy a crib."

He shook his head. "It took me some time to get used to the idea. But it's for the best. Lily needs a place of her own to sleep. It's silly to let the crib, the furniture, the toys just sit there when they're needed."

Again the room was still, and Jenna's unasked questions about the accident somersaulted like clowns in a circus in her mind. She did her best not to voice the questions, but it sure wasn't easy. If Gage wanted to talk, he'd talk. If he didn't, it was his right to keep his story to himself.

He'd told her plainly how he felt early on. He'd agreed to help her with her problem. He hadn't agreed to open up his life to her.

Just when it seemed that he intended to keep his private life private, he set his mug down on the table and sighed.

"It was a car accident." His gaze locked on something across the room, while his thumb smoothed the ceramic handle of his coffee mug. "Mary Lynn, my wife, was driving our sedan. I was in the passenger seat. Our daughter, Skye, was in her car seat in the back."

He paused, every muscle in his body strained. After he swallowed, he quietly continued, "It was a beautiful, sunny day. Not a cloud in the sky. We weren't traveling at an excessive speed. There was absolutely no reason to suspect that our trip home from a day of shopping in Billings would turn into the worst nightmare of my life."

Jenna sat still and breathless. She knew firsthand what heartache and devastation a car accident could bring. A split second could forever change lives and alter the future.

"I still can't say what kind of animal it was," he said. "A mink. A weasel. A muskrat. All I saw was a flash of dark fur on the road. Mary Lynn swerved. I can still hear her tiny squeal in my head. It was something she did when she was surprised. She jerked the steering wheel too sharply. Jammed the brakes too hard. They locked up is what the state trooper told me later. All I know is that the rear of the car fishtailed. Violently. We struck a cement median. And then we were airborne. Tumbling. The car rolled at least once and landed on its roof."

Sometime while he spoke, he'd laced his fingers around the coffee mug. Jenna noticed that his knuckles had gone pale with the force. She hoped the ceramic didn't crack under his nervous strength.

"I walked away with barely a scratch. Mary Lynn and Skye were dead before I could get myself out of the car and get to them."

Compassion impelled Jenna to reach across the table and slide her fingers over his forearm. He seemed to relax under her touch.

"It was an accident," he told her. "A freak accident. No one was at fault. There's no one to blame. It's just that—" he inhaled deeply "—I can't help but feel guilty. For surviving."

Jenna's heart pinched in her chest.

When they first met, he'd seemed like such a hard man. Unfriendly. Surly, even. But now she was learning that he was just like her. Very human. Nursing wounds of grief and guilt. Trying to get through the best way he could.

She was acutely aware that her hand was still on his

arm, so she pulled it back, curled her fingers and placed her fist in her lap. "I think what you're feeling is perfectly natural."

After a moment, he said, "I'm sure you're right." He reclined against the chair back and took a drink of coffee. "I should have cleared out the nursery months ago, I guess. It's been a year. I just haven't been ready." His tone went soft as he added, "I'm still not ready."

He seemed more relaxed, and Jenna couldn't help but ask, "How old was she? Skye?"

Surprisingly, he smiled. "She'd had her first birthday a month before the accident."

"Oh," Jenna breathed, "so little." Her spine straightened as she was struck with a startling realization. "Lily must—"

Remind you of Skye, was what she'd been about to say.

So much made sense to her now. His initial refusal to marry her so she could gain custody of Lily. His tense attitude when they'd picked up Lily from Arlene's house. His long hours spent out in the stable. His unwillingness to have anything to do with her niece.

He hadn't been avoiding Lily. He'd been avoiding memories of the daughter who had been taken away from him.

"I want you to know—" a slight quiver changed her voice "—that I'm very grateful to you for all you've done for me and Lily. You've done something amazing, having us here, in light of all you've been through."

"I'm just repaying a debt."

She couldn't help but smile. "I understand that's how you see it. But from where I'm sitting…" Suddenly, words failed her and a nervous tension flared inside her like a bright flame. She was overwhelmed by his graciousness. He'd agreed to have her and Lily in his home even though doing so was sure to stir his memories of the past.

"But why now?" she asked. "Why open up the nursery? Why tell me about the accident? You made it pretty clear before that you wanted to keep your private life to yourself."

"I don't think any of us could have gone another night without sleep, do you?"

She averted her gaze. She had no idea what kind of response she'd expected from him, but for some reason his answer left her feeling a little chilled.

What had she hoped he'd say? That he'd come to trust her? That he'd suddenly decided she was worthy of his secrets?

That was silly. How could he have come to trust her when they hadn't spent ten minutes alone together? For four days she'd been busy inside the house with Lily and he'd kept himself busy outside.

Okay, so he'd offered the use of the nursery because Lily needed a crib. End of story. And he'd told her about his wife and daughter because…? Well, she guessed it was because he felt he needed to explain why a man living alone would have an immaculate nursery.

The whys shouldn't really matter to her, should they? The fact that he'd confided in her meant a great deal. It changed her opinion of him. It made her see him in a whole new light.

She understood him a little better now. *No,* a silent

voice in her head corrected, *she understood him a lot better now.* The warm emotion gathering in her chest took her off guard. However, what started out as a pleasant sensation quickly turned so troubling that she felt a tiny frown mar her brow.

When she'd asked Gage for his help, she'd never expected to feel compassion for him, or empathy for his situation. Those feelings could be dangerous; could turn into something else—something more intense, more intimate. Yes, a woman could all too easily fall for a man like Gage.

Marrying someone completely unfamiliar to her in order to get custody of Lily had seemed harmless when she'd devised the scheme. But this marriage of convenience didn't feel so safe anymore. Her frown deepened. After experiencing Gage's kindness last night, after hearing his tragic story this morning, she could no longer call her husband a stranger.

Chapter Five

"May I join you?"

Gage's question had Jenna twisting around to find him standing at the back door. She smiled. "It's your back porch."

The springs of the screen door creaked as he stepped outside. "You looked as if you were deep in thought, and I wasn't sure if I should bother you."

Well into her second week of living under Gage's roof, Jenna was pleased with the way things were going. Lily seemed to have settled in. Jenna was actually getting a little work done. And Gage had finally been able to relax around the baby.

"I just tucked Lily in for the night," she told him. "I've got work to do, but I slipped out here to enjoy the quiet for a few minutes. You're welcome to join me."

He sat down on the porch step next to her and immediately she was aware of the heated scent of him. She had noticed that Gage didn't wear cologne very often. Not that she'd wanted to notice. She simply couldn't help herself. And she had come to the realization that, for some reason, she found his fresh, soapy smell more enticing than the most expensive aftershave.

"The sky is beautiful tonight," she said.

"I never get tired of staring up at those stars."

"I can't help imagining that some jeweler tossed a palmful of diamonds across rich black velvet." It wasn't like Jenna to be so fanciful, but she was in high spirits.

She and Lily had enjoyed a day of fun and play. Lily was sleeping soundly now, and Jenna had finally been able to finish updating a particularly complicated Web site. The job had taken her days longer than she'd anticipated, the baby needing her undivided attention whenever she was awake. But Jenna had accomplished the task, so she was feeling pretty good.

"How was your day?" she asked. "Did you get everything you needed in town?"

"I did. I'm sorry I was late getting back."

Jenna suppressed a smile, hoping the darkness would cover the humor bubbling up inside her. What a difference just two short weeks made. When she'd first arrived, he'd been crabby and short-tempered and never around, and now here he was apologizing to her because he hadn't arrived home exactly when he'd said he would. Anyone listening in would have thought they really were a married couple.

"I found the leftover pot roast in the fridge," he said. "It was good. Tender and tasty. You're a great cook."

"Thanks. I was forced to learn a few domestic skills pretty early."

"Oh?"

Jenna looked out into the night and listened for a second to the hum of flying insects, the soft chirp of crickets.

"When I was twelve, my mom cut herself and went to a doctor in Rock Springs for stitches." The memory had her mouth flattening and she smoothed her splayed palms down her thighs. "She didn't keep the wound clean and developed a staph infection that invaded her bloodstream. It ultimately took her life."

"That's terrible," Gage said.

She nodded. "Amy was nine when Mom died and, being the oldest, I felt I had to take over Mom's responsibilities. My dad had never been a very good provider. He did what he could, but he had a tiny drinking problem." In truth, her father was a flagrant alcoholic. "He floundered from job to job." She shrugged. "So I did what I could to keep the household running. When cash was low, I found odd jobs that would earn a little bread money."

"Must have been tough."

She swiveled her head to look at him. "You do what you have to do. I'm sure lots of people have had it harder than me and Amy. At least my dad kept a roof over our heads while we were growing up."

"Is he still in Rock Springs?"

"He died two years ago. His liver was in bad shape."

Gage's expression filled with sympathy.

"So, with both your parents gone, I guess you and Amy were close."

Jenna nearly winced. "Not as close as we should have been. We didn't agree about her education. I wanted her to attend classes at community college. We couldn't afford tuition at a bigger school, and her grades weren't good enough to earn any academic scholarships. That really didn't matter because the idea of going to college didn't appeal to her, anyway. All she was interested in was painting. However, that didn't keep me from harping on the subject. After one particularly loud argument when she was eighteen, she packed her things and left home. She ended up in Chicago. I would hear from her now and then, but one day she called to say she was moving back to Montana. That she'd met an artist named David Collins and they were getting married.

"They moved to Broken Bow where David was certain things would be economical for them. And it was. They were happy here. And I liked having Amy close again."

Gage was quiet a moment, then said, "Well, I know a little about your sister, but what about you? Since education seems so important to you, were you able to attend college?"

Self-consciousness forced Jenna to look away. "I took a few courses, but not nearly enough to earn a degree."

He chuckled. "So you wanted your sister to do as you said and not as you did."

She grinned sheepishly. "Something like that. But I found my niche very early."

"Your computer work?"

"Yes. I'd just graduated from high school, when the local public school system refurbished its computer labs. They gave away lots of computers, and one of them landed in my hungry little hands. I took a couple of computer courses, and I talked the local bakery into hiring me to build them a Web site. They really didn't expect anything to come of it." She lifted one shoulder a fraction. "And to tell you the truth, I didn't, either. But soon they were sending cookies and cakes and bread to places all over the U.S., not to mention Japan and England and Germany. Delicious Desserts is still one of my clients. I'm proud to say that I've built a pretty lucrative business."

However, the lessons she'd recently learned were heavy enough to round her shoulders. "But it came at great cost."

His raised eyebrows were a clear sign that he was curious for more information.

"Amy and I had done without for so long," she continued, "that once I started making money, all I wanted to do was make more. When I wasn't on the computer building sites or learning how to create even more intricate graphics, I was networking and querying, always trying to increase my clientele. It seemed that, in the blink of an eye, Amy had grown up and then she was gone. But I never slowed down. My engine was stuck in high gear, and I kept my nose to the grindstone." She rolled her eyes and quipped, "Mixed metaphors. Anyway, I thought I had forever to fix my relationship with Amy. Although we did see each other a little more often once she returned to Montana—especially after Lily came along—it seemed that everything still took second place to my business." She shook her head. "I have to admit, I had worried about finances for so many years that it wasn't so much building the business as earning money that had become important."

"I think that's a normal reaction, Jenna. You grew up worrying about having your basic needs met. It's quite natural to want to see to it that you have enough income to survive."

Although she appreciated his commiseration, she turned away and said softly, "Yeah, well, in one brief phone call from an E.R. nurse I learned that I didn't have forever with Amy."

His eyes were on her. She didn't have to turn her head to know. She could feel the intensity of his gaze almost as if it were a tangible thing.

"That's why getting custody of Lily was so crucial to me." She couldn't say why she was explaining the motivation behind her actions in such detail. It could be that after two weeks with little to no adult company, she was itching for some conversation that didn't necessitate a cutesy baby tone. Then again, it could be that she simply wanted Gage to know her a little better.

The implications of *that* surprising thought filled her with a strange, almost giddy excitement.

But whatever the reason, it seemed all-important for him to understand what drove her to make a marriage bargain with a perfect stranger, to pick up and move to Broken Bow Reservation, to change her whole existence for one tiny child.

"I've learned a very hard lesson," she continued. "Life can change in the blink of an eye." She was well aware that fate had taught him that same lesson, as well. "Family is more important than a career, or money, or anything else. And I want to spend every day showing Lily what I made the mistake of not showing Amy. That I love her and care about her. Above all else."

"She can't help but know that." His voice was as sultry as the summer night. "It's obvious that you're dedicated to her."

The discomfiting feeling of being scrutinized swept over Jenna. She'd talked about herself enough.

"And you're mighty dedicated to this ranch and those horses out there," she observed. "You put in really long hours."

Two weeks ago, she never would have made a comment so blatantly geared toward getting him to talk about himself. However, since the night he'd offered Lily the use of the nursery—and told Jenna why he'd been so reluctant to invite the baby into his home—he'd been more laid-back, more open. Visibly so, actually. He still had moments that were tough for him, Jenna could tell. But he was reaching out more and more to Lily.

"I have some really big shoes to fill," he said. "My dad started the pinto breeding business. And he worked extremely hard to build something for his children. He was married to his first wife for nearly fifteen years. When no children came along, the woman divorced him. So my parents were in their early forties when they met and married and had me." He grinned as he added, "At least once a year I hear the story of what a great blessing I am to them…usually on my birthday."

"Family stories can get old after a while, but I don't believe that one would," Jenna said.

He chuckled. "You're right. Anyway, when Mary Lynn and I married three years ago, Dad and Mom were ready to retire. They bought an RV and spent a good year traveling. They've visited every state in the continental U.S. They fell in love with the Arizona desert and because the dry climate was good for Mom's arthritis, they decided to settle there.

"I could never leave. I love this place too much. The ranch, the horses." His gaze meandered toward the stable. "I knew from the time I was a boy that I'd make this my life's work."

The moment stretched and Jenna thought he'd revealed all he meant to. But then he leaned over, resting his elbows on his knees.

"I nearly lost the place when Mary Lynn and Skye were killed," he said. "Before then, I had twice as many horses and I had a couple of hired hands working full-time to help me take care of things. After the accident—"

He dropped his head, the thick curtain of his hair falling over his shoulder. Jenna marveled at how the moonlight reflected, blue-black, against it.

"I just didn't have the same…I don't know…initiative, or energy, or something."

"You were dealt a mighty blow, Gage."

His spine straightened. "I could say the same for you." He turned his head then, and captured her with his gaze.

A tingling sensation started low in her belly and

spread outward into her limbs. Her muscles felt as if they were reaching some sort of melting point, and she was so glad she was sitting down. A potent force emanated from him, a formidable energy that drew her to him.

Dear Lord! She was attracted to Gage Dalton.

It wasn't as if she had no experience with men. Okay, so she didn't have a lot. And at twenty-six, she just might be the oldest virgin in the entire state of Montana. But she had dated some. Okay, she had a repertoire of exactly three. But two of the relationships had lasted several months, and one had lasted off and on for nearly a year.

However, she hadn't gotten close enough to any of her boyfriends to entrust them with any kind of true intimacy. And not a single one of those men had stirred in her the physical reaction that Gage had with just one look.

Self-consciousness forced her to lower her gaze. "I— I guess it's s-safe to say we've both been wounded." She hated that she'd stammered. "But we're survivors, right?"

She bolstered the question with a small smile, but still she couldn't bring herself to look him in the face again just yet. She needed to regain her composure first. She needed to deal with the realization that he roused in her some incredibly compelling corporal responses.

"If that's what you want to call what I've been doing for the past year."

The pessimism in his statement took her aback. Lifting her chin, she made direct eye contact. "That's exactly what I'd call it." Her tone was resolute. "People survive the best way they can. You've kept the ranch going. And I've put every ounce of my energy into Lily. We just have to hold on, Gage. We have to trust that things will get better. Easier. That the night won't be so dark. We have to have faith that the sun will rise, and that a new day will come."

Her face flamed when she saw that her corny spiel had him grinning. His chuckle only increased her embarrassment.

He splayed his hands on rock-hard thighs. "Now *you* sound like one of the Wise Ones."

"The who?"

"The Elders. They're famous for diminishing one's troubles with encouragement. And they usually have a great folktale to go along with it. That kind of thing is a fundamental part of the Lenape culture."

Her embarrassment quickly turned to discomfort. "I would never profess to being wise. But there's nothing wrong with encouraging someone when he's down, is there?"

"No," he said. "Not a thing."

She loved the rich resonance of his voice.

"Since you've raised the issue of the Lenape culture," she said, "I'd like for you to tell me a little about your history. As a tribe, I mean. If, that is, you're not too tired."

"I'll tell you anything you want to know."

"I have to admit," Jenna said, "I don't know very much about Native American history. I remember learning about the Trail of Tears in high school. I understand that Indians were forced off their land when the Europeans arrived in droves. But other than that..." She lifted her hand, palm up. "It's kind of embarrassing, actually. That I'm not more knowledgeable about American history. But after my mother died, I was too busy after school doing laundry and cleaning and cooking to do much reading."

Understanding softened his black-as-midnight eyes, affecting her in a way that made her avert her gaze.

"The Lenape weren't involved in the Trail of Tears," he told her. "That event marked the displacement of our Cherokee brothers. In 1838, the entire Cherokee Nation was made to march a thousand miles from their home in Georgia to the government-decreed Indian Territory in Oklahoma. The conditions of the trip were deplorable, and over four thousand Cherokee died before they reached their destination. The actual Cherokee translation for the trek is 'Trail Where They Cried.'"

Chagrin once again heated her face, supplanting the sadness the story stirred in her. "I'm sorry if it sounded as if I was lumping all Indians together. I wasn't being rude. Not consciously, anyway. I do realize there are different Nations of Indians. Even different tribes within each Nation. I know that Montana alone is home to Blackfeet, and Sioux, and Crow, and Cheyenne—"

"It's okay, Jenna. I wasn't insulted."

She clamped her lips shut, hoping the awkwardness she felt would pass.

"The Lenape's westward move began just under a hundred years prior to what you know as the Trail of Tears."

"A hundred years *before?*" She couldn't keep the surprise and indignation out of her tone. "Those early settlers didn't waste any time taking what they wanted, did they?"

She suspected his smile was in appreciation of her righteous anger on the behalf of the plight of all Native Americans.

"I think our suffering came because we happened to live on the land closest to the first colonies. It took longer for settlers to filter north into New England and south to Georgia, the Carolinas and Florida.

"In all fairness," he said, his tone a smooth baritone, "our oral historians have always claimed that William Penn dealt fairly with my ancestors. But after Penn returned to England, his agents began to sell land in order to pay their debts. Unfortunately, the land they were selling was home and hunting ground to the Lenape."

He inhaled, and Jenna couldn't keep her eyes from lowering to his broad chest.

"You have to understand," he continued, "Indians had no concept of owning and selling land. The idea was as ludicrous to them as selling air. Land belonged to the Great One."

Jenna offered, "Kit-tan-it-to'wet."

He nodded. "The Creator provided land for his children to hunt and fish. My ancestors simply didn't understand the notion of possession. And they were taken advantage of because of that.

"Penn's men cooked up a crooked deal as a means of convincing my forefathers to give up the land. The agents found an old, unsigned deed and presented it to the Lenape leaders as a legal contract. They claimed that fifty years before, our ancestors had signed this agreement handing over to the government as much land as could be covered in a day-and-a-half's walk. It became known as the Walking Purchase."

"The document was completely bogus?"

"It was. But not knowing that, the Lenape felt honor-bound to respect the deal made by their ancestors."

Jenna murmured, "The crooks lied."

"The story gets worse. The Lenape leaders agreed to allow the area to be 'walked,' thinking that Penn's agents wouldn't be able to cover more than two or three miles. Instead, the agents had a straight path cleared. And they hired three runners. By the time all was said and done, the so-called walker who had covered the most distance had gone fifty-five miles."

The unscrupulousness made Jenna shake her head.

"Penn's agents acquired twelve hundred square miles of Lenape homeland that day," Gage continued. "An area about the size of Rhode Island. And for the next one hundred and thirty years we moved time and again, our clans broken up and scattered like wheat kernels on the wind. My ancestors ended up here, on Broken Bow Reservation."

"I think it would be wonderful to know where I come from as well as you obviously do," Jenna said. "I mean, I know my mother's parents were Dutch and my father's were Irish. But that's all I know." She tucked a strand of hair behind her ear. "I like the way your tribe keeps its traditions and holds on to its culture."

Gage twisted his body to rest his back against the porch post. Jenna was well aware that now he didn't have to turn his head to look at her. That should have bothered her, made her feel exposed. But she realized she liked having his undivided attention.

"Traditions are good things, don't get me wrong," he said. "But we'd be foolish not to take full advantage of all the technological advances that have come along. Still, forgetting where you come from is never a good thing. We do our best to remember our past. There are powwows and other celebrations that feature traditional music and songs and food—"

"Are any of those things happening soon? I'd love to go."

He went still.

"What is it?" she asked. "What did I say?"

"It's nothing." He reached over and plucked a long blade of grass that grew by the porch step. "It's just that it's been quite a while since I've attended any of the tribal gatherings."

Since he'd lost his family. Jenna didn't have to ask. She just knew.

"Maybe it's time for that to change."

There it was again. That amazing—nearly over-whelming—energy pulsing from him, drawing her in. Like invisible fingers plucking and pulling at her.

"Maybe." Leisurely, he wrapped the long blade of grass around and around his finger.

"I—I mean," she stuttered, suddenly nervous as a rabbit caught in the crosshairs, "I'd really like to attend. So I can show the Elders that I'm taking care of things. You know, that I intend to do what's right…learn what I can about your tribe. And I don't know that I'd feel comfortable going without you."

For some odd reason, that statement only made her all the more anxious. Her tongue darted across her cottony lips. This man shoved her off-kilter even during casual conversation. "Of course, we'd be going for Lily."

His eyelids lowered in a slow and deliberate blink. "Of course," he said. "For Lily."

Chapter Six

The door of the self-storage unit creaked as Jenna opened it. A breath of dry heat smacked her in the face. Nerves jittered in her belly like tiny fingers of dread tinkling out sour notes on piano keys.

"You sure you're ready for this?" Gage asked.

"Don't know," she admitted honestly, grateful to have him with her. "But I do need to look around. At least a little."

Having left Lily with Arlene for a couple of hours while she and Gage took a look around the storage facility, Jenna propped open the door allowing the summer sunshine to stream into the dark recesses. She stepped inside and searched for the light switch.

The bare overhead bulb cast stark light down on the stacks of cardboard boxes all neatly taped and labeled.

"Looks organized," Gage observed.

"It does, doesn't it?" She inched along the narrow aisle that ran through the piles of boxes. "The Elders took care of cleaning out the house. They asked me if I wanted to do it—and I did—but they wanted it done immediately."

"The tribe owns the house?" he asked, evidently realizing the situation.

Jenna brushed a smudge of dust from her trousers. "Yes. Amy and David rented from the tribe. And from what Amy told me, the rent was nominal."

"There are many such houses on the rez. It's my understanding that the waiting list to get into one is long."

Jenna nodded. "I was annoyed that the Elders were pushing me to make a decision about my family's belongings. They were rushing me, I felt. I was going through so much. Fighting for Lily. Planning the funerals. David's parents are both frail and pretty much left both burials to me."

"You had a lot to deal with."

The deep concern in his tone made her halt her forward movement and she glanced at him. Empathy softened his features. She smiled, feeling less alone than she'd felt in a long time.

"Not that I'm complaining," she said. "I was happy to be able to honor my sister and her husband's life together." Memories of the day she buried Amy and David crowded into her mind. "I planned a very simple service. I don't have any real family to speak of, and David's parents didn't say how many people they expected to attend. I probably should have asked. But I was amazed at how many people came to the service. Apparently, some of them traveled long distances to attend."

"That doesn't surprise me. Remembering those who have returned to the ancestors is an important part of our culture."

Absently, Jenna smoothed the pad of her thumb along the edge of a cardboard box. "Before the caskets were closed, David's mother covered my sister and her son with these gorgeous blankets she'd made. It's something I'll never forget.

"And at the cemetery, people offered the most beautiful gifts. Jewelry, a perfect white feather, a silver mirror, a stuffed animal. One young man actually left money."

"Offering gifts is our way."

"But money?" She couldn't rein in her astonishment. "As we left the cemetery, I saw faded bills tucked next to many of the headstones. It's a wonder the cemeteries aren't looted."

"No one would ever dare disrespect the dead or the gift givers. Those offerings are made out of honor and love and remembrance."

"It was all so touching. And afterward—" she shook her head in wonder "—I couldn't believe the meal that just seemed to materialize. We'd gone back to David's parents' house, and it seemed like close to a hundred people were milling around inside and out. Tables and chairs appeared. And plates laden with chicken and ham and roast beef. Casseroles of every vegetable imaginable. I hadn't planned any of that. It just…appeared."

He nodded, clearly unsurprised by what she'd learned was Indian custom.

Jenna combed her fingers through her hair. "I hadn't meant to bring all that up. Thanks for listening to me ramble. I don't know how I got so off track. I was just trying to explain why I didn't have it in me to tackle the job of packing up the house back then."

She sighed. "However, as exasperated as I was with the Council, I did understand their need to get the house ready for new renters. So I agreed to allow them to oversee the job." She smiled ruefully. "I have a feeling they would have done it even if I hadn't agreed."

"Probably," he agreed softly.

"I made arrangements for this unit and the movers brought everything here. There's supposed to be a typed inventory somewhere."

"I'm sure it will turn up."

Jenna turned and made her way farther down the aisle. She saw boxes labeled by room and contents.

Kitchen: Small Appliances

Kitchen: Cutlery

Living Room: Knickknacks

Sighing, she plunked her hands on her hips. Eventually, she'd have to sort through everything, of course. Some items she'd keep for Lily. But she'd have to get rid of much of the stuff. Jenna couldn't see Lily ever needing or wanting a twenty-year-old clock radio or electric can opener.

But for the life of her, she couldn't imagine disposing of anything that belonged to her sister and brother-in-law, be it a can opener or a dry, crusty paintbrush. Not just yet. The grief in her was still too raw. But surely that would change. She hoped and prayed it would. Surely, time had a way of, if not healing, then at least lessening the pain of one's wounds.

Time. That was what she needed.

Her gaze fell on a box near her feet marked Master Bedroom: Family Photos and Albums. Without allowing herself to think about it, Jenna bent over and peeled up one corner of the tape. She gave a quick and forceful jerk and the box flaps came free.

There on top were two framed snapshots. The first one, faded with age, was a black-and-white image of Amy as an infant. A three-year-old Jenna cradled her new sister in her arms while their mother beamed at them.

The second photo was much more recent. Amy sat next to Jenna on a sofa, newborn Lily snuggled between them.

As she stared at the pictures, powerful emotions rumbled within her like so much thunder. She squatted down, resting her bottom on a cardboard box, and let emotion engulf her.

Gage made his way back from the far side of the storage unit where he'd wandered through the sea of brown boxes. He'd called Jenna's name to say he'd made a startling discovery, but when he turned to find her, she was nowhere in sight. It wasn't that the unit was all that huge, but many of the stacks reached near ceiling level.

He found her hunched near an open box. Whatever it was she'd found seemed to hold her mesmerized.

Although she'd clearly displayed herself as a strong woman in the weeks she'd been under his roof, he'd also discerned vulnerability in her. A vulnerability she was loath to show. It was that tiny glimpse of defenselessness, he believed, that stirred his response to her. His urge to protect her.

Of course, any man with a heart beating in his chest, with blood running through his veins, would respond to this woman. Her brown eyes were expressive. Her shiny auburn hair lured a man to explore its silkiness. And her delicate features would entice even the stoniest of men.

It wasn't as if he'd never encountered a beautiful woman before. But Jenna was more than that. For some reason, he wanted to wrap his arms around her and tell her that everything was going to be okay. He wanted to keep her safe from harm. Wanted to make her smile.

However, some self-preserving intuition told him that the desires she churned in him were dangerous to his well-being.

Even when he crouched beside her, it was clear that she was oblivious to his presence. Peering over her shoulder, he spied the family photos she held in her fingers.

He touched her upper arm and she gasped softly, her golden-brown gaze flying to his.

"I called you," he said.

"Sorry." Her cheeks flushed and her gaze returned to the pictures. "I guess I got wrapped up in the past."

Her light floral perfume floated on the still and dusty air, and an overwhelming impulse struck him. But he battled the itch to lean even closer, to press his nose to her warm skin and inhale the scent of her deep into his lungs.

Jenna placed the framed photos back in the box with what he could only describe as a gentle and loving hand.

Tipping her chin up, she asked, "Could we take this box with us when we leave?"

The despair coursing through her was laid bare, leaving her open. Exposed.

"Of course." The compulsion to shelter, to protect, hit him with astonishing strength. He knew the sadness of losing a loved one. If he could take that away for her, he would.

Then the emotion pulsing from her transformed, and Gage sensed that the heartache she'd suffered just an instant before dissipated to be replaced by something different…something perilously risky.

Desire.

He had the amazing sensation that he'd reached some sort of fork in the path of his life, a significant juncture that had the potential to forever alter his existence. His thoughts were whirling too fast for him to figure out the what, why and how of the moment. He only knew this instant, this event, was important.

Her soft lips glistened in the light cast by the bare bulb overhead. She pursed her mouth slightly, seeming to beckon him silently to act. Then her eyelids fluttered closed. His heart hammered, his blood slogged through his body.

Dark lashes fanned against creamy skin that he easily imagined would be satiny soft. Helplessly, he reached out to run his fingertips along the rise of her cheekbone, down the fine curve of her jaw. At his touch, her nostrils flared a fraction when she inhaled deeply, expectantly.

Her breath quickened, her chest rising and falling. The swell of her breasts pressed against the cotton fabric of her top, and he ached to smooth his hands over their ripeness, feel their weight in his palms. But instead, he merely let his fingertips travel down the length of her throat. Her hot pulse throbbed against his skin. He stopped at the curve of her collarbone.

The rational part of his brain went to war with the desires of his body. Hunkered down next to her, he prayed for the conflict to come to some resolution. He thought his pause was merely momentary. But evidently it had been much longer than he thought because she opened her eyes, her questioning gaze clashing with his.

Discomfort settled over him, and he wanted to apologize to her. For what, he couldn't quite say. For not kissing her? For not tugging her down and taking her right there on the gritty concrete floor?

"It's all right."

Her voice sounded husky and sexy as hell. He knew his brow was knit with bewilderment as well as indecision.

Slowly, confidently, she ran her tongue over her bottom lip. "Nothing may have happened just now," she said, her tone so low it was nearly a whisper. "But I think we just experienced a momentous event."

A delicious tingle ran down his spine when she chuckled.

The momentous event, he suddenly realized, was that both of them were fully aware of the sexual temptation each posed for the other.

"Jenna—" her name rasped from his throat as if his larynx had turned into a rusty spring "—I, um, I'm not looking for this…well, for this kind of…"

"It's okay," she assured him once again. "It really is okay, Gage."

He hated that he felt so awkward when she seemed so cool…so at ease with this strange turn of events.

Not that he hadn't wanted her before this moment. He'd felt drawn to her from the very first. He'd admired her strength. She hadn't blinked an eye about taking on the Elders in order to acquire custody of Lily. She'd uprooted herself and changed her whole life in order to do what she had to do for her niece. And he'd be lying if he said he hadn't noticed her physical beauty. Yes, she had roused in him needs that were perfectly natural. But he'd been able to rein in his feelings. Until now.

He gulped in air, instantly desperate to focus on something—*anything*—else.

The artwork. Of course. That was why he'd come looking for her to begin with.

"I found something," he said. He rose to his feet. Held out his hand to help her do the same. "Something I think you'll want to see."

She slid her palm against his, curled her fingers and gripped tightly. The heat of her caused a hitch deep in his gut. The instant she was standing, he released his hold on her.

"This way." He turned and weaved through the boxes toward the left wall of the storage room.

Gage knew the instant Jenna saw the canvases by her sharp inhalation.

"My God," she whispered, her tone awed. "I expected to find artwork among Amy and David's things, but I never expected anything like this. There must be two hundred pieces here."

He pressed himself against a wall of cardboard so she

could get a better look. As she passed him, he was too aware of the feminine scent of her, a fragrance evoking the image of walking through a wildflower meadow on a hot summer day.

He said, "I haven't checked carefully, but it looks like there's more stacked against the back wall."

While Jenna busied herself looking over the art collection, Gage allowed himself to study her.

Astonishment sparkled in her golden gaze and flushed her lovely face, making him remember the softness of her skin against his fingertips just moments before.

The fact that he'd reached out to stroke her face troubled him a great deal. Why had he acted on the urge to touch her this time when he'd been able to subdue all impulses before today?

When he'd approached her, she'd been engrossed in those pictures. Engrossed in the past. Engrossed in a moment of time spent with her sister that would never and could never be repeated. She'd looked distressed and... vulnerable.

"These are wonderful!"

Evidently, the surprise she felt was giving way to excitement. He was relieved to see a smile light up her beautiful face as she momentarily glanced his way.

"I can't allow this stuff to stay hidden in here," she told him. "Amy and David would want their work seen. Enjoyed. I've got to find some way to make that happen."

She went back to investigating the canvases.

Pleasure arrowed through him when he realized she was no longer focusing on the sadness of the past, but was instead enthusiastically concentrating on the future.

"You'll think of something," he murmured.

He pressed his lips together, troubled by the hot and unmistakable desire that once again curled low in his belly. He reminded himself that it was Jenna's vulnerability that was affecting him so deeply.

He scrubbed his hand across the back of his neck, suspecting that there was more to what he was experiencing than he was willing to admit. But he staunchly stomped the idea as if it was some sort of bug under his boot.

Normally, he wasn't a man who lied to himself. He believed that a person who traveled through life ignoring the truth was in jeopardy of losing his true self.

But the thought of shining a light on the reality of his situation made him too nervous. He just wasn't ready. Every time he imagined himself getting involved with a woman again, the guilt lying dormant like so much silty sludge would churn and eddy, muddying his thinking. Besides, it wasn't as if his rationale was a complete fabrication. Jenna *was* vulnerable. And he *did* identify with the anguish she was experiencing. His wanting to comfort her didn't make him a bad guy.

Okay, so maybe he was focusing on only half of the truth. But it was all he could handle. For now.

"I'll bring your order shortly." The teen smiled politely and then backed away from the table.

Gage had agreed with Jenna's suggestion to have lunch at Hannah's Home-Style Diner after they picked up Lily from Arlene's house. The baby sat in a high chair at one end of the table, happily gnawing on the floppy ear of a light blue stuffed elephant.

"Thanks for going with me today." Jenna unfolded the linen napkin in front of her and laid it on her lap. "I felt as if I'd stepped onto a roller coaster—down one minute while I was lost in memories of my sister, and up the next while I was looking through her and David's artwork. I think it would have been worse for me if I had been alone."

However, the wild emotional ride she'd experienced hadn't been caused solely by sorting through Amy's and David's belongings. Gage had done more than his fair share of rousing her feelings, as well.

"I was happy I could be there with you."

She watched his calloused fingers fidget as he shifted first the saltshaker, then the pepper shaker, then rearranged the small plastic container that held sugar packets. She remembered the feel of his work-roughened skin against hers when he'd caressed the side of her face. The hunger in his black eyes had pierced her to the very marrow of her bones. The memory alone made her stomach thrill with delight even now.

She guessed the wise thing would be to ignore the feelings throbbing through her. She sure didn't need another complication in what was already a complicated mess—lying to the entire Lenape Nation about why she'd married this man. Besides, she would bet her last dollar that Gage would rather grab the molten end of a fiery-hot poker than surrender to the obvious attraction swirling around them. He just wasn't the kind of man who gave in to temptation easily. That was why she'd been so stunned when he'd done just that. She still couldn't believe he'd actually reached out to her.

But she also hadn't been the least bit surprised when his fingers had stilled, when he'd restrained his thoughts, his emotions, his desires. His entire body had tensed when he'd withdrawn, and then he'd pretty much told her that acting on their attraction had been a mistake.

"Hi, Jenna. Gage." A smile spread across the face of the Native American woman who approached their table. As owner of the diner and Arlene's daughter, Hannah Johnson had become somewhat of a friend to Jenna during Jenna's battle with the Council of Elders. "How are you folks today?"

"We're just fine, Hannah," Gage said. "How about yourself?"

"Oh, I can't complain. Are you coming to the Stomp Dance?"

Gage's dark brows rose. "I hadn't heard about it."

Excitement spread across Hannah's beautiful face. "You've got to come. Now that you're married, it's time for you to stop hiding from us." Her tone softened as she added, "It's time you made peace with your grandfather, as well. It's silly that the two of you live so close, yet continue to let the wall of silence between you stand. Knock it down, Gage. It would be easy enough to do."

Jenna quickly hid her surprise. She'd had no idea that Gage had a grandfather living on Broken Bow, or that they weren't speaking.

"What's silly—" Gage's dark gaze glittered with a good-natured cheer "—is that you honestly believe I'll take your advice."

Hannah chuckled. "Isn't there an old adage that says keep banging them over the head and someday the message will sink in? Come on," she coaxed. "Come to the dance, at least. Jenna needs to experience a gathering."

"I'd love to go," Jenna said.

"It's this Saturday," Hannah told them. "People will start congregating early, I'm sure, since they'll be coming from miles around. But dinner won't be served until six. It's a potluck, so bring your appetite and a dish of some sort to share. Doesn't have to be fancy. There'll be a bonfire once the sun goes down. There'll be music. Plenty of dancing. And storytelling, too. You'll have fun."

Hannah's dark eyes filled with concern as she changed the subject. "I heard you were over at the storage unit this morning. You okay?"

Jenna hoped the smile and nod she offered would set Hannah's mind at ease. "I left Lily with your mother. Did she tell you where we went?"

"I knew Mom was watching this cute thing—" Hannah ruffled Lily's hair eliciting a gleeful gurgle from the happy baby "—but I've had three different customers who stopped in this morning mention that they'd seen Gage's truck out at the self-storage place. I just hope you weren't too upset."

It warmed Jenna to know she had people who were concerned about her. "I'm okay," she said. "I had a somber moment or two. That's to be expected, I guess. But I wasn't alone. Gage was right there with me."

Jenna gazed gratefully at Gage, and had to suppress her grin when she saw that he looked ill at ease.

"It's good to have someone to share those kinds of things with," Hannah observed. She patted Gage on the shoulder. "You're a good guy."

He *was* a good guy, Jenna realized. Going with her on her trip to the storage unit wasn't something he'd had to do, yet he hadn't hesitated to offer his support.

"I found lots of artwork," Jenna told Hannah. "One thing I learned today is that my sister and her husband were very prolific."

"Are you going to sell it?" Hannah asked.

"I haven't had a chance to think about it," Jenna said. "I sure can't leave it where it is."

"I agree," Gage said. "It would be a shame if all that work was left hidden away in that building. I mean, David Collins had several shows in Chicago, didn't he? And you said that he and your sister would want people to enjoy their art."

"Jenna," Hannah said, "why don't you ask the Council if you could display David and Amy's work in the Community Center? You could even post prices on them. Or you could place some of the pieces on consignment with an art gallery in Billings. Heck," she continued, "you could contact a Chicago gallery for that matter, to see if they'd be willing to sell the work for you."

"A gallery would expect a hefty cut of the profits, I'm sure," Gage warned.

The idea of selling the artwork set Jenna's thoughts churning. "A Web site," she murmured. "I could create a Web site with pictures of all the pieces." Her excitement intensified as ideas continued to come to her. "In fact, I could make a Web site to accommodate all the artisans here on Broken Bow. There have to be other artists on the reservation."

Hannah's face lit up. "There are. John Riddle makes

beautiful pottery, and his wife weaves baskets in the authentic Lenape fashion. There's a woman who still makes hide clothing—dresses, capes, trousers. I don't know if that's considered art, but I fear that'll someday become a lost skill. My cousin, Lisa Johnson, paints. So does Harold King. I'm sure there are others, as well."

At some time while Hannah spoke—Jenna couldn't be certain exactly when—Gage had slid his hand across the table and rested it on her forearm. The warmth of him slowly permeated her consciousness, and her gaze swung to his.

There was something unreadable in his eyes. An expression that made her breath hitch in her throat. Her mouth suddenly felt dry.

"I think a Web site is a wonderful idea, Jenna," he said.

"Oh, I think so, too." Hannah babbled on about how Jenna's project would benefit the people on the rez, evidently unaware that the temperature of the diner seemed to have increased by ten full degrees in as many seconds.

Jenna's mind had been filled to the brim with plans one moment, and completely empty and incapable of reason the next. Gage's strong, tapered fingers on her skin consumed her, and an unexpected delight flooded her being. She smiled at him, an errant thought making her wonder if he'd found her brainstorm so amazing that he'd forgotten his declaration about not wanting a relationship with her.

Just then, the bells connected to the front door jangled, signifying that a new customer had arrived.

Jenna swiveled her head and watched Hoo'ma enter

the diner. The elderly woman nodded toward Jenna and Gage, approval glittering in her wise eyes.

"Hoo'ma! Welcome!" Hannah greeted the elderly woman. "You've come for lunch?"

Hoo'ma nodded, her papery eyelids fluttering in a blink.

Hannah looked at Jenna. "May I tell her about your idea?"

"Of course," Jenna told her, still wrestling with the immense internal emotions swimming in her chest, pounding in her head.

Hannah crossed the room, chattering brightly about the Web site and Jenna's inspired idea to introduce the world to Broken Bow's artists.

"I'm…sorry," Gage murmured, leaving his hand on her forearm but staring at the spot where his skin made contact with hers. "I saw Hoo'ma coming across the street through the front window. I thought it would be a good thing if she were to see us, you know…as an affectionate couple."

"Of course," Jenna murmured a second time. It took her a moment to figure out just what was happening. But the instant she did, huge disappointment crashed over her.

Just a few seconds ago, she'd been unable to decipher the expression on his handsome face. But now she could clearly recognize his apprehension, his reluctance, his uncertainty. Why hadn't she been able to see it before?

"I thought this…demonstration—" his gaze darted again to the place where his hand rested on her forearm "—would be a good thing." Then he leveled anxious eyes onto her face once again.

"Of course," she repeated. She felt like an idiot who had only two words in her vocabulary.

"I hope I did the right thing."

He was a good guy. Hannah had said it, and she'd silently agreed. He'd been putting on a show for Hoo'ma in order to make their sham of a marriage look more legitimate. For her to have imagined there had been anything else motivating him had been stupid of her. Especially after he'd come right out and told her at the storage building that an intimate relationship didn't interest him. Well, he might not have proclaimed those exact words, but that was what he'd meant. How could she have so quickly forgotten? Why did she feel such disappointment?

He was a good guy. Jenna needed to remember that. That and that alone was the force driving his words and actions.

His being a good guy wasn't a bad thing. She wouldn't want it any other way, would she? Besides, hadn't she decided that an intimate relationship would only complicate her life?

"Of course," she whispered, uncertain if she were responding to Gage, or to her own silent, taunting questions.

Chapter Seven

Several days later, Gage suggested they pack a lunch and take a gentle horseback ride out to the far meadow. At first, Jenna had balked, fearing the idea of Lily on one of those huge animals.

"Don't worry," he'd assured her. "I have a cradleboard. And I'll carry her. She'll be fine." Then his dark eyes had narrowed. "You're not afraid to ride, are you?"

Jenna had chuckled. "Maybe a little."

He'd promised to saddle his most docile horse for her. And he'd been true to his word. With their lunch packed in saddlebags and Lily safely stowed on the cradleboard secured to Gage's broad back, they set out across the green meadow.

Riding a few steps behind him, Jenna couldn't help but notice how the worn denim of Gage's jeans molded to his thighs, or how his hips undulated in the saddle in conjunction with each step his horse took, or how he carried Lily on his strong back as if she were featherlight.

Because she understood his wish not to act on the attraction that tugged at them, Jenna had been determined to ignore it. Sometimes, ignoring temptation was easy. Those were usually the days when Gage was busy in the stable or one of the other outbuildings. But even when he was out of the house, she found herself peering out the window, hoping for a glimpse of him even though she knew full well she shouldn't. On other days, the attraction was so strong that Jenna ended up exhausted trying to act as if it didn't exist. As if the kinetic energy between them hadn't turned the very air into a giant vortex bent on carrying them toward its mysterious yet alluring center. Unfortunately, today was one of those days.

She wondered what it would be like to smooth her palm over the hills and valleys of muscle on his bare back, skim her fingers down his spine—

She wasn't able to stifle the gasp that had lodged in the back of her throat.

"Everything okay back there?" he asked, glancing quickly over his shoulder.

"Fine. I'm fine. How much farther?"

"Not far." He reined his horse until they were side by side. "You sure you're okay?"

"Yes. I'm a little tired, and I can tell my legs are getting quite a workout."

"See the tree by the stream?" He indicated a spot ahead with a gentle jerk of his chin. "That's where we're headed."

At the end of the twenty-or-so minutes it had taken to ride what Jenna estimated to be another mile, her thighs and buttocks were screaming. She dismounted clumsily and couldn't hold back the tiny *oof* that escaped her lips when her feet hit the ground

If Gage had attempted to restrain his chuckle, he failed. He swung his leg over the saddle and descended to the grassy meadow so smoothly that Lily barely stirred. The gentle motion of the pinto had rocked her to sleep.

"I'll need some help with this." He unfastened the buckle at his chest and turned so Jenna could ease the baby off his back. "Loosen up the lacings," he suggested, "and lay her down in the shade."

While Jenna untied the rawhide cords and pulled back the soft doeskin cover that held Lily to the cradleboard, Gage busied himself unloading the food and picnic essentials from the saddlebags.

Jenna placed her niece on the blanket he spread out. "This contraption—" she leaned the cradleboard against the tree "—is just marvelous."

"Indian women in the past would use them to carry their babies around as they tended their chores or worked in the fields. It left their hands free." He unbuckled the second saddlebag and started emptying the contents. "That one was made for me by my father. I got to use it when Skye was born. Not many people continue the tradition, though. The plastic and canvas carriers they make these days are much lighter, and a lot less expensive."

"Not to mention easier to get," Jenna said. She handed him a prepackaged moist cloth. After cleaning her hands with one herself, she placed a sandwich and napkin in front of him and then served herself. "All you have to do is visit the baby department at your local variety store. How long does it take to make a cradleboard, anyway?"

"Weeks, I'm sure. But I've never made one. My dad is very good with his hands. He can make anything."

The lightness in his tone made her want to smile. Gage liked his dad. That was clear.

Sunlight streamed through the leaves overhead, dappling the ground beneath. The brook gurgled over and around smooth stones, making delightful and calming music. He'd chosen a lovely spot for their picnic.

She poured them each a glass of cool juice from the thermos. "Speaking of family, do you mind if I ask what's going on between you and your grandfather? Hannah said the two of you weren't talking." She pinched off a corner of her bread and popped it into her mouth.

Gage unwrapped his sandwich. "I don't mind talking about it. I'm upset with Grandfather because he made my parents feel guilty for moving to Arizona. He wanted them to stay here. On the rez. But my mother's got arthritis, and the dry, warm climate there is better for her."

He bit into the ham and cheese sandwich, chewed and swallowed. "I understand that Grandfather is our shaman. And it's his job to—"

"Chee'pai?" Astonishment made her sit up straight. "Chee'pai is your grandfather?"

"Yes."

"Why didn't you say something before? You knew I was butting heads with the Elders."

He only shrugged. "Wouldn't have done any good. It didn't surprise me, though, to learn that he was the main reason the Council was refusing to give you custody of Lily. He is very concerned with the tribe. He wants to keep us together. He wants things to remain the same. And although it's a noble cause, I fear it's impossible. This isn't the old days, and the old ways don't work for everyone. He hurts people with his harsh words, even though his intentions are pure."

Jenna remembered her arguments with the Elders. Chee'pai hadn't really hurt her feelings. But he'd certainly ruffled her feathers and frustrated her to no end.

"Will your grandfather attend the celebration on Saturday night?"

Gage nodded. "He will be part of the storytelling. As hard as he is, I have to admit he is a gifted orator."

"If you'd rather not attend—"

"No, no," he said, swiping his mouth with the paper napkin. "I'll go. Like Hannah said, I have to make amends sometime. And it's not as if Grandfather changed my parents' minds. They're happily settled in their new home. It's high time I set things right with him, I think."

Lily showed great timing by sleeping until Jenna had swallowed the final bit of her juicy apple. But once the baby opened her eyes, she let everyone know she was hungry and ready for some attention.

Jenna sat her niece on her bottom, opened a jar of strained peaches and started spooning the fruit into Lily's mouth.

"It's so easy to make her happy." Jenna shifted her

position, stretching out her legs. The muscle cramp in her calf made her suck in her breath.

"What is it?"

"A charley horse, I guess," she said. She rested the spoon in the jar of baby food and reached down to rub her leg. Lily fussed.

Gage came to her rescue. "You feed. I'll rub."

The feel of his hands on her knotted muscle was both heaven and hell. His fingers were warm even through the fabric of her jeans, but the pain of the spasm made her frown as he massaged deeply.

"It'll go away in just a second," he assured her. "I promise."

She managed to smile through a grimace, and he chuckled. Jenna resumed feeding Lily, guiding the spoon into the baby's mouth, again and again, until she scraped the bottom of the empty jar. Lily gleefully snatched the spoon, waving it in the air like a baton and then tapping it against the sole of her sneaker. Jenna set the empty jar aside, sighing when—true to his promise—Gage finally kneaded away the knotted cramp in her calf.

"Oh, my," she breathed, "that's much better."

She leaned back, resting her weight on bent elbows. She glanced down the length of her body and their gazes didn't just connect, they melded. Desire blazed in his expression, in every tense muscle of his body.

His hands spanned her calf, although his fingers were now still. The heat of him was amazing. Even the rays of the summer sun beating down on her weren't as hot.

Her breathing quickened. So did her heart rate.

There was nothing mysterious about what tightened

the air. He wanted her. That was as clear as the cloud-less sky above.

"I'm sorry," he murmured. "I don't know what's wrong with me."

Jenna couldn't stop herself from asking, "Why do you see it as something wrong? What we're feeling is completely natural. We may not want to feel it, but we're feeling it just the same."

His features went taut.

"I should be able to control myself."

He shot to his feet then, and walked away from her. He stood at the bank of the creek and scrubbed his hand across the back of his neck.

Jenna marveled at how a fabulous day could turn bad so quickly.

It couldn't have been more obvious that he didn't want to want her. And he didn't want to talk about it, either.

Well, she'd do what she could to accommodate him.

"Gage," she called, "come on back over here. This is no big deal." That was a whopper of a lie if she'd ever told one. But if he was determined to ignore the fire be-tween them, she would, too. "Let's clean up this mess and go back home."

The evening of the Stomp Dance, Gage made a quick stop at the outbuilding he used as a workshop before heading toward the house to shower and dress. The boxes he carried contained gifts—one for Jenna, one for little Lily. He felt self-conscious about giving them, but he intended to give them, nonetheless.

Having Jenna and her niece in his house for the past

three weeks had changed his life. Changed his outlook. Changed *him*.

The changes were both good and…not so good.

He awoke each morning feeling that the day held promise. He felt bright. Eager. Content. He actually looked forward to getting up and experiencing all that was in store. He guessed what he was feeling was hope.

He hadn't felt that in a very long time.

He'd once dreaded the idea of having Lily around, fearing that her presence would stir his grief for his own little girl. Instead, what he'd discovered was that Lily awakened some extraordinary memories—of hearing Skye's bubbly laughter, seeing her wobbling on all fours for the first time, smelling the baby powder-fresh scent of her after her bath, feeling her chubby little fingers curl securely around his.

In mere weeks, Lily had unearthed a treasure chest of precious moments spent with Skye that had been buried beneath a mountain of heartache and anguish. So Gage planned to give Lily a small gift to honor what she had done for him. To show his appreciation. Being so small, she wouldn't understand it, of course. But that didn't matter. All that mattered was that he offered her the tribute she was due.

Jenna deserved a tribute, too. For she had unearthed something in him, as well. She had exhumed a raw need in him that he'd thought he would never again experience. Not reacting to it—to her—was probably the most difficult thing he'd ever done. But he was determined to ignore the desire she sparked in him. Because he just wasn't ready.

However, the gift he carried to the house for Jenna was motivated by gratitude. The day he'd lost his family, his soul had been crushed. For a year, he'd wallowed in self-pity, in anger, in a multitude of dark emotions. Without his even realizing it, Jenna had been coaxing him out of the darkness. And for that he was thankful.

He heard music playing before he reached the house. He smiled, anticipating Jenna's excitement about tonight's celebration. She'd been looking forward to experiencing a tribal gathering. She was also eager to show the Elders her willingness to learn and participate in the culture.

He wiped his feet on the mat, pushed open the door and saw Jenna dancing around the kitchen with a laughing Lily perched on her hip. So caught up in the music and the steps, Jenna didn't even know he'd entered the house.

Her auburn hair hung loose about her shoulders, and happiness pulsed off her. Lily giggled. He stood there watching them, waving at the baby.

In his mind's eye, he easily conjured an image of Mary Lynn dancing in a similar way with his precious Skye. He smiled. His heart pinched, but at the same time the memory brought him immense pleasure. It was nice being able to think about the past without being swallowed by despair.

With all his heart, he believed Jenna and her niece had made all the difference.

"Hey," he greeted.

Jenna actually yipped, her eyes widening in surprise as she spun to face him.

"I didn't hear you come in," she said.

"That's obvious," he commented with a laugh. He glanced down at the boxes in his hands, then took a step forward, intent to offer the gifts before he lost his nerve. "I have something. Something for you. And Lily."

Unmitigated delight brightened her already flushed and joy-filled face. His entire body responded to her beauty; his chest went tight, his muscles tensed, and he was inundated with an amazing and permeating heat.

He looked away from her, sucking in a cooling breath as inconspicuously as possible. The instant he felt that he'd garnered control, he lifted his gaze and offered her both boxes.

Jenna accepted them, sliding her palm beneath them, but they proved too unwieldy for her to manage with one hand. She tipped her hip toward Gage and Lily automatically reached out her hands to him.

He took the toddler and Jenna took the boxes in one smooth exchange.

Immediately, Lily curled her fingers in his hair. She seemed fascinated with it and played with his hair whenever she got the chance. She was always gentle. And he didn't mind. In fact, he enjoyed feeling her tugs and twirls.

Jenna opened the smaller box, the one sitting on top, and gasped. "They're so cute," she breathed, pulling out the tiny moccasins. "Lily, look!" She lifted the doeskin booties for the baby to see. Lily clapped and then reached out for what she determined was a new toy.

"We're going to put these on your feet, sweet stuff," Jenna told her, setting the larger box on the table so she could tug off her niece's tiny sneakers and slip on the moccasins.

"I hope they fit," Gage said.

Automatically, Lily began kicking her feet joyously and peering downward to stare at her new shoes.

"They fit fine," Jenna announced. "And she loves them. Can you give Gage a kiss?"

The toddler's kiss was more like a wet nibble on the corner of his jaw, but his chest filled with emotion. "I'm glad you like them," he told Lily softly.

Jenna reached for her box. "Can I open mine now?" she asked.

He nodded.

Her reaction this time was less animated, but nonetheless sincere. "They're beautiful, Gage." She ran her fingers over the top of the moccasins. "The beadwork is so delicate. They must have been very expensive. Where did you get them?"

"I made them."

The wonder reflected in her eyes made him puff with pride.

"My grandfather taught me to make moccasins when I was a teen," he told her. "As kids, we're disciplined to avoid idleness. Encouraged to find productive hobbies." He shrugged. "I stopped the hobby for a while, but went back to it after the accident. I needed something to fill the—" he stopped suddenly, moistening his lips and swallowing "—something to do with my hands." He pulled in a breath. "I have quite a few pair out in the storage building."

"What are you going to do with them?"

He shrugged. "I have no idea."

He could see that her mind was working.

"Could I offer them for sale on the Web site?" she asked.

"People aren't interested in—"

"Oh, but they are! I've been doing some research while putting the site together." She held the moccasins gingerly, as though they were precious jewels. "Native American items are very hot sellers. Shoes like these would bring a hefty price."

"But I don't need the money. Like I said, it's a hobby. Something to fill my idle time."

She lifted one shoulder a fraction. "Then donate the money to the Community Center."

He blinked. Then he nodded. "Okay. If you think the moccasins will sell."

Jenna grinned with confidence. "I know they will." Then she turned her sparkling honey-brown eyes on Lily. "We're going to fit right in at the Stomp Dance, aren't we, sweet stuff?"

Delicious aromas and lively music filled the air as they arrived at the dance. Gage told her that after dinner had been enjoyed, the sun had set and the bonfire blazed, the more modern instruments—guitars and fiddles and electronic keyboard—would be replaced with the more traditional drums and wind flutes.

A long row of tables had been set up, and they were laden to groaning with food of every description: succulent fried chicken, pulled pork and barbecued beef, baked beans, corn pudding and green beans simmered with bits of smoked ham, mounds of asparagus marinated in spices, flatbreads and corn muffins. Jenna set down the platter of still-warm molasses cookies she'd made to share.

Gage, Jenna and Lily sat on the grass and ate their fill. Then they moseyed through the crowd, listening to the music, visiting and enjoying themselves. Gage introduced her to some of his friends. They chatted with Arlene and Hannah, who just happened to be munching on a couple of Jenna's cookies.

Eventually, the sun lowered beneath the horizon and the first stars began to twinkle. Several men rallied a group of teens who stacked wood for the bonfire. Once the blaze was ignited, Jenna felt a renewed excitement zip and snap in the air.

The sky turned a deep mauve. Wisps of plum-colored clouds floated high overhead. Stillness settled over the crowd. It was as if everyone knew something amazing was about to happen.

The drummers began to pound out a haunting rhythm, and a lone figure danced through the people, and around the fire. A carved mask covered his face. He wore an elaborate outfit—a long headdress enveloped with pristine white feathers, a tanned vest and trousers, beaded moccasins.

Gage leaned close to Jenna, whispering, "That's Grandfather."

His breath was like velvet against her cheek.

"As our shaman, it is his duty to start the festivities."

The elderly man made a bending and wide scooping motion with one arm, then the other, then lifted his hands toward the sky, never missing a single intricate dance step. For a few moments, she lost sight of him as he moved to the far side of the blaze. But before too long, he came back into view.

"He is honoring our ancestors," Gage said. "He is letting them know we remember."

She watched Chee'pai dance, then glanced around at the enthralled expressions of the crowd. Young and old, men and women—all those assembled seemed to be recalling a far distant time.

A chill coursed through Jenna as she was struck by an amazing revelation. The shaman worked diligently, not just tonight but every day of his life, doing all that was in his power to preserve the treasure with which he'd been entrusted. The treasure that was the Lenape legacy.

She remembered the story Gage had told her about how the land had been stolen, about how the very honor of the Lenape tribe had been used against them, about how they had been offered one promise after another only to see each one broken, about how they had been pushed westward, again and again.

Yet, they had survived.

Even though the shaman hadn't spoken a single word, it was clear to Jenna now that Chee'pai—and every single person attending tonight's gathering—felt it a great privilege to be called Lenape.

No wonder the shaman had ranted so during the Council meeting about the young people leaving the reservation. No wonder he'd been so adamant that Lily remain on Broken Bow. No wonder he'd gone to the trouble of teaching his grandson how to make moccasins.

He was only doing his job. He was trying to protect that which he held sacred. The tribe.

Gage had tried to tell her all those weeks ago. But it seemed she'd had to figure it out for herself.

By the time the first dance of the evening ended, Jenna had tears in her eyes. She also had a new respect for Chee'pai.

"You seem lost in thought."

Concern softened Gage's onyx eyes.

She smiled and nodded. "Yes. It's just overwhelming…all of this."

Her statement seemed to bewilder him, and she suspected he was going to ask her to elaborate, but the drummers began pounding out a new beat. And the crowd stirred.

Arlene approached them. "It's the Women's Dance," she said, touching Jenna's arm. "Would you like to join us?"

"Oh, no." Jenna would have backed away if she could. "I'm just here to watch tonight, if that's okay."

Hannah joined Arlene, excitement lighting her gaze.

"Is she coming?" Hannah asked her mother.

"Not this time." Arlene looked at Jenna. "Can we take the little one?"

Hannah laughed. "Yes. Miss Lily wants to dance."

"Of course." Jenna handed Lily over to Arlene who danced to the beat toward the other women in the clearing. Even Hoo'ma joined in the festivities, lifting her skirt an inch above her bony knees, tossing back her head and stepping to each thundering punch of the drum.

Emotion welled in Jenna's chest, knotted in her throat. "This is wonderful," she said to Gage. "All of them know the steps. All those women out there seem so…connected. I want Lily to be a part of this. For always. It's like…well, look at them…it's—" She stopped, so overwhelmed that words failed her.

"We're one big family," Gage provided.

She nodded, not trusting herself to say another word.

He took her hand. "Come on. Let's go find something cold to drink. I think you need a break."

They walked in silence away from the crowd, and Jenna was grateful that Gage was giving her a few moments to pull herself together. Finally, she gazed out toward the horizon and took several deep breaths. His fingers curled tighter around hers as she garnered control of her emotions.

"Better?" he asked.

She nodded, sensing that it wasn't necessary for her to speak.

Remembering how prickly Gage was when they'd first met, she marveled at how comfortable she'd become around him. She liked him. She more than liked him. And not because he was probably the best-looking guy she knew. Or because, with his broad, strong shoulders, his lean torso and powerful thighs, he had a body that wouldn't quit.

No, it was more than that. She'd discovered that he was interesting. And kind and caring. And intelligent.

Whoa, girl! a silent voice warned. *Keep this up and you're going to talk yourself right into love.*

No way. That wasn't going to happen. Gage wasn't interested. Not in anything permanent. And judging from the way he worked so hard at disregarding the attraction flitting around them like fireflies on a summer evening, Jenna knew he wasn't even interested in anything fleeting.

Gage halted his steps before they reached the area where the coolers were stored. He spun her around to face him.

"You're a special woman, Jenna Butler," he murmured.

Shocked speechless, she gazed up into his face.

He'd released her hand and was now smoothing his palms up her arms, over the curve of her shoulders, caressing the arch where her throat met collarbone. He stared down into her eyes, emanating a magnetism so strong, it was nothing short of magical.

She blinked once, twice, three times, finally grasping that Gage most definitely felt the urge to kiss her.

And this time, he fully intended to act.

Chapter Eight

His mouth slanted down over hers, ardent and demanding. He slid his arms around her, pulled her to him, his strong hands splaying against her back. Enveloped by the heated scent of him, Jenna closed her eyes and relaxed against his chest, parting her lips in an invitation he readily accepted.

He explored with his tongue, nibbled with his teeth, suckled with his lips. Jenna felt light-headed as passion consumed her. Blood whooshed through her ears, her pulse pounded, her heart hammered, nearly drowning out the sound of the drums as her body thudded with a primordial beat all its own.

The roughness of the kiss was just what she wanted, just what she needed, to release the craving she'd confined for far too long. A craving he'd obviously confined, as well. Beyond containment, it now seemed.

He trailed hungry kisses along her jaw. Jenna heard her own shallow and panting breaths.

A flash of fear splintered through her brain. What if they had become a spectacle?

The wild question forced her eyes to open. The first thing she realized was that they were in the shadow of a towering hemlock. She glanced toward the crowd, and relief weakened her knees when she saw that everyone had their backs to them, intently watching the Women's Dance.

She let her eyelids flutter closed and relished the feel of Gage's mouth on her skin. His tongue traced a fiery trail to her earlobe. He kissed it, then pressed his lips to her temple. He ravaged her with his kiss, and it was all she could do not to whimper with need. She wanted to unbutton her blouse. She wanted to tug off his shirt. She wanted to feel all of his bare skin against her own.

She whispered his name against his lips, understanding that every desperate emotion rushing through her was conveyed in her husky tone.

He pulled back just enough to gaze down into her face, and Jenna resisted the urge to reach up and touch her fingertips to her moist, tender, deliciously bruised lips. Desire blazed in his black eyes. The yearning raging through him honed the planes and angles of his face.

He wanted her. She felt it in the heat that radiated off him in waves. Heard it in his ragged breath. Felt it as the apex of each quick inhalation brought his chest tight against her breasts. Her nipples budded in response, hardening to sensitive nubs beneath the thin cotton of her top.

"Sweet heaven, Jenna."

He wanted to look away from her, she sensed. But for some reason, he couldn't.

"I don't know what came over me. I—"

He stopped, ran his tongue over his already moist and luscious bottom lip.

"I'm sorry."

Sharp disillusionment doused the flame of her passion, and she took a deep breath. Although he hadn't thought to release her yet, she knew the heated moment was over.

"I know exactly what came over you," she said, her words shaky. "It was the same thing that came over me." Her chest heaved with another deep breath as she slowly shook off the amazing emotions that had captivated her…that had captivated them both.

She tipped up her chin boldly. "I'm only sorry that you're sorry."

As if on some strange cosmic cue, the drums ceased and the air went still for the span of several heartbeats while Jenna held Gage's gaze. She stepped away from him then, realizing that what she was feeling was regret.

But how could that be? she wondered. She didn't want an intimate relationship with Gage. She'd already decided that in her mind.

He'd already decided that with his words.

Confusion knitted her brow.

"I don't need a drink right now," she told him. "What I need—what we both need, I think—is some space."

She walked back toward the crowd to find Arlene, Hannah and Lily.

Gage chugged the springwater straight from the bottle he'd plucked from the cooler. The icy liquid cooled his throat, but did little to douse the embers of lust still burning low in his belly. That was what he was feeling for Jenna, he was certain. Plain old lust. Closing his eyes, he pressed the cold, wet plastic against his forehead.

Annoyance tensed his jaw until his back molars ached.

He wasn't a randy teenager. He should be able to control himself. His body. These damned inappropriate inclinations.

But they were becoming stronger and stronger. And Jenna had looked so sweet watching her niece participate in the dance with the other women of the tribe. The idea that the Lenape people saw themselves as one huge family was a revelation that had genuinely hit home with Jenna tonight. She'd nearly become overwhelmed with the realization. He hadn't meant to take advantage of that. Not by any means. But he'd gotten swept up in the moment. He'd have to be more careful not to let that happen in the—

"Grandson."

Gage jerked his head up and saw his grandfather standing beside him. The elderly man had taken off his ceremonial headdress. Chee'pai bent over, reached into the cooler and picked up a bottle of water.

"It is good to see you here," his grandfather said. "It's been a long time since you've attended a gathering."

Thinking about how this man had hurt his parents' feelings, Gage stewed in silence for a moment. But then he remembered what Jenna had said about family. Life could change in the blink of an eye. It was time to set resentment aside and do what he could to heal old wounds.

"I'm enjoying myself tonight," Gage said. "I had forgotten how fun—" he checked himself the instant he realized his word choice didn't quite capture his full intent "—how important it is to get together. It's good to see old friends again." Pointedly, he added, "And family."

"It is good." His grandfather nodded. "I've missed you."

"And I've missed you."

The two men clasped each other in an immense bear hug, and Gage's heart warmed.

"Did you see that Jenna is here with her niece?" he asked.

Disapproval flattened his grandfather's mouth. "I saw. But she does not fool anyone. Just as a feather cape wouldn't make a fox an eagle, a pair of fancy moccasins doesn't make her Lenape."

Gage squared his shoulders. "She's not trying to become Lenape. The shoes weren't even her idea. I gave them to her this evening."

Chee'pai looked skeptical but remained silent.

"She really does want to learn about our culture," Gage said. "So she can teach Lily about her heritage."

"That child should be raised by her paternal grandparents. They're Indian. They would give—"

"David Collins's parents are old," Gage pointed out, knowing full well that interrupting his grandfather was terribly rude. "And they're sickly. They're not able to take Lily in. They're not able to keep up with a toddler. Jenna is. Besides that, she loves that child. Why are you so against her?"

He knew full well the answer to his question. He even understood his grandfather's thinking. He just didn't agree with the logic that the People had to remain in a close-knit pack like a family of wolves. If Jenna took Lily away from Broken Bow, that would not make the child less Lenape.

If…?

Gage looked off into the darkness, suddenly astonished. His use of *if* rather than *when* meant that he thought there was some uncertainty about Jenna's leaving the reservation. How and when had he come to that conclusion?

"My grandson," Chee'pai said, breaking into Gage's deep and startling thoughts, "there comes a time when everyone must learn that love isn't always enough. That child needs more than Jenna Butler's love. And I'm going to see that Lily Collins gets everything she needs to become Lenape."

In Gage's mind, Lily didn't need anything from his grandfather to become Lenape. She already was Lenape. But voicing that would only further irritate his grandfather, and Gage had come to the gathering tonight with the thought of smoothing their relationship.

However, he couldn't help but correct one misstatement. "She's not Jenna Butler. She's Jenna Dalton."

His grandfather swiped at his mouth with the back of a weathered hand. "That is something that has been troubling me. Why would you marry that woman? If you decided so suddenly that you needed a wife, there are plenty of single women here on the rez. For instance, Hannah Johnson has never been married—"

"Grandfather, stop." Gage lifted his hand. "The choice of who or who not to marry was mine to make. And it's a choice you must learn to live with."

"And I could do that if I believed for one second that your reason for marrying that woman was honorable."

Ire flared in Gage. "My reason *was* honorable."

The elderly man's brows rose skeptically. "You've been holed up on your ranch ever since the accident. You left for business and for supplies. Period. There was no time for you to meet a woman. And I know your heart has not healed enough to develop a relationship, loving or otherwise. I came out there to visit you, remember. I know how you were feeling. No one could break through that wall of grief. Granted, I am an old man, but I am not easily fooled."

Gage clamped his lips tight. His grandfather might be stubborn, and narrow-thinking, but the man was also astute. Telling his grandfather that he and Jenna were in love would have been an outright lie that would bring shame on his name and on his people. And the truth— that he was paying back a Life Gift, even though it was completely respectable, in Gage's mind—would only offer his hard-hearted grandfather more fodder for his bad feelings against Jenna.

Bending down, Gage snatched up another bottle of

water, and then leveled his gaze onto his grandfather's. "Nothing I have done would bring my family shame. The arrangement Jenna and I have is our business. Now, if you'll excuse me, I want to bring my wife something cold to drink."

"Can't sleep?"

Gage's question had Jenna turning from where she'd been staring out the kitchen window at the moonlit meadow.

She shrugged. "I was tossing and turning. I finally just got up. You okay?"

When he opened the fridge, light spilled across the floor. "Just thirsty," he said, pulling out a jar of apple juice.

This sparse, artificially bright repartee set Jenna's teeth on edge. It was how they'd addressed each other ever since the night of the dance over a week ago—ever since that instant of surrendered passion in the shadow of the towering hemlock.

That kiss had changed everything. Before that moment, they had slowly developed a real relationship, had become friends of a sort. Yes, that hum of attraction never failed to present itself when they were together, but they'd done a fairly good job of ignoring it. Gage had stopped hiding out in the stable and outbuildings, filling his time with work, and had actually seemed to enjoy spending his evenings with Jenna and Lily.

But since they'd spent those fiery moments in each other's arms, he'd once again retreated from her.

Who was she kidding? She'd done her share of retreating, as well. But she'd had plenty to occupy her time—spending her days with Lily, keeping up with her business clients and creating the new Lenape artist Web site by night.

She had to admit she was quite content to keep busy. Her schedule left little time for sleep. And that was okay. Sleep was something else she'd started to avoid. Well, not sleep, exactly. What she was desperate to escape were the dreams. Hauntingly seductive visions of Gage running his bronze hands over her milky body, kissing her with explosive passion, pleasuring her all through the night. She'd awaken each morning with a desolate feeling, a needy ache that refused to go away.

One of those night fantasies had jolted her from sleep over an hour ago. She hadn't been able to find a comfortable position after that. Thoughts of Gage had refused to be banished and had finally chased her out of bed. She'd been keeping vigil at the kitchen window ever since.

She watched him pour juice into a glass and lift it to his lips…the same lips she fantasized about in her dreams.

Moonlight glowed against his white T-shirt. When he leaned to set the empty glass on the counter, a thatch of his dark hair fell across his well-defined biceps.

The alluring current between them buzzed around her so loudly, it sounded like an agitated bumblebee. She wished it *were* an insect, something she could swat at and shoo away. But this was a temptation that refused to be expelled.

"Your meeting go okay today?" he asked.

Jenna nodded. She'd met with the Council and with a small group of artists who lived on Broken Bow.

With Lily propped securely on her hip, Jenna had stood in front of the room and explained her ideas for the Web site, listed her requirements regarding images she could upload and announced the date she hoped to launch the site. They batted around ideas, talked about how to split the proceeds and what to do with the tribe's share. Jenna quickly learned that it was the Lenape way to always give a little something back to the People, so she offered to donate a portion of any money she made on her sister's and brother-in-law's artwork.

"They agreed with my idea of naming the site Foxfire. In David's memory. Everyone seemed excited," she told him. "Everyone except your grandfather." She sighed. "I've come to the conclusion that nothing I do will ever make him happy."

Gage reached up and hooked a hand behind his neck, the action tightening the corded muscles of his forearm. Jenna had to concentrate in order to keep her gaze on his face.

That ever-present energy they conducted raised the hairs on her arms, made her skin feel all prickly and too aware.

"He's a hard man to please."

Gage pressed one lean hip against the edge of the countertop and crossed his arms over his chest. Again, Jenna had to work hard to keep eye contact with him when all she really wanted to do was let her gaze drift down the full length of his body.

"You've been working late into the night all week," he commented.

There was true concern in his voice, real interest. Something she hadn't heard for days. It took her off guard.

"I've heard the tap of your keyboard. Seen your light on. Often until long after midnight."

All she could do was nod in response. She wanted to ask what he was doing up so late, but didn't.

The buzzing tension amplified. Gage's intense stare clearly told her he was cognizant of it.

"Jenna, we need to talk."

He didn't need to tell her what he wanted to discuss. She knew without a doubt what the topic would be.

"I agree," she said.

His jaw muscles tensed, then relaxed. He licked his lips. He uncrossed his arms. "This...*thing*—" he lifted his hands, his fingers curling as if he were attempting to grasp some unseen object "—between us. It's very powerful."

Jenna felt an immense pressure on her chest and wondered if it was nerves, or curiosity, or anticipation. Her voice was very small as she murmured, "I certainly can't argue with that."

He swallowed and remained silent a moment or two, his bottom lip captured between his teeth. She got the sense that he was choosing his words, measuring them, trying to decide exactly what to say.

"I felt this...thing," he continued, "from the very first." He paused long enough to take a deep breath. "The attraction, I mean. I feared it, in fact. But then I decided I could disregard it. I *would* disregard it. I could act as if it wasn't there." He rubbed his fingers over his jaw. "But it...the stirrings...they're often...stronger than me. Stronger than my resolve." His black gaze latched on to hers. Earnest and earthy. "Like…right now."

Jenna's knees went weak as she nodded her complete understanding. Something twittered in the pit of her belly. "I know what you're saying." The words grated against her dry throat. "I fought it, too," she told him. "I thought I didn't need any more complications than I already had. And I knew you weren't interested in…that you didn't want—" Unable to complete the thought, she lowered her gaze. "But…sometimes…the feelings I have are…overwhelming."

A taut silence settled over them.

Finally, Gage said, "I understand and empathize with your not wanting to add to your problems. You've got so much that you're dealing with right now."

She lifted her head to see some bleak emotion flash across his countenance. Pain? Anxiety? She couldn't say.

"I loved my wife, Jenna," he said, his tone jagged, as if the words themselves had been cut with a dull serrated knife.

Her heart wrenched close to the breaking point for him. That short profession revealed so much. He felt guilty for wanting her. He thought the attraction he felt for her somehow lessened the love he'd shared with his wife.

Jenna went to him, reached up and pressed a tender palm to his cheek. "You can't think like that, Gage. What you and Mary Lynn had was special. It will always be special. Nothing you can ever do, or feel, or say will ever change that. Nothing." She paused, wanting to let him know how emphatic she was about what she felt was the honest truth.

"But at the same time…" She stopped, suddenly inundated with a myriad of emotion. "At the same time, you have to remember that you're human. It's completely natural for you to have needs. Physical wants and desires."

The swirling current grew more fluid. Like some warm, smooth, thick liquid, it eddied all around them. On a breathy whisper, she added, "Just like everyone else."

Then she took a moment, inhaling shakily as she garnered the courage to verbalize her thought wholly and more clearly. "Just like me."

She let her fingers trail slowly down his neck, then she flattened her palm against his chest, never breaking eye contact with him. She had figured out very early on that Gage harbored a wounded heart. Well, she had the chance to help him heal. Right here. Right now.

The look she offered him was an obvious, even brazen, summons. A call that needed no words to be understood. When she raised on tiptoe to kiss his mouth, she had no clue how he would react, or what he would think of her. Would he think her shameless? Wanton?

If he did, that would be all right. Because right at this moment that was exactly how she felt.

Lifting his hand, he trailed his fingers up her arm, his skin barely touching hers, and she got the impression that he was toying with the idea of submitting to the temptation purring and pleading for attention.

"Let go of control," she told him. "Tonight, I want to be your soft place to fall."

She reached down and slipped her hand beneath the hem of his T-shirt, the need to touch him becoming more than she could bear.

He was a good man. An honorable man. A man who fulfilled his word. He'd sworn to repay his debt by helping her, and never once had he faltered in that promise. For that, she would be eternally grateful.

For that, she wanted to show her thanks.

His belly was warm under her fingertips, his abdominal muscles rock-hard. He sucked in a short breath, and for an instant, she feared she'd upset him, crossed over some obscure boundary he'd drawn. But the potent emotion she read in his onyx eyes had her mouth curling languidly, sexily. Her brash behavior surprised him, and she liked the idea that she could shock him. Liked it very much.

Slowly, she gathered the soft cotton of his shirt in her hands, tugging it up and over his head before letting it fall to the floor.

Her gaze raked down the length of his lean, hard torso, taking in his nipples, dusky brown coins against his bronze skin, his firm pecs, his defined abs. His belly button riveted her eyes. The tiny fold of skin mesmerized her. It was more erotic than it had any right to be.

Her heart pattered in her chest and she had trouble breathing. She felt the urge to gulp in huge amounts of air. She felt another urge, as well. The urge to taste.

She bent and placed a kiss by his belly button. Parting her lips, she dragged the tip of her tongue against his flesh. His skin was velvety smooth and hot. He inhaled a long ragged breath and triumph rushed through her whole body. He cupped the back of her head with his hand, lightly massaged her scalp.

His pajama bottoms rode low on his narrow hips. She

was struck with the impulse to slide her fingers beneath the elastic band, to tug and pull, to see him completely naked. But there was plenty of time. She wanted to go slow. She wanted to savor every touch. Every kiss.

She wanted her first time to be special.

With nimble fingers, he caressed her chin, and gently guided her upward until they were once again standing face-to-face.

"Are you sure about this?"

His question vibrated with such thoughtfulness that Jenna feared she might tear up. Never had she met a man so considerate.

She opened her mouth, but found that she was so affected by the moment—by him—that she was unable to speak. Wanting him to know she was completely clear-headed about what was about to happen, she forced herself to say, "I've never been more sure of anything, Gage."

She leaned against him then, lifting her chin, and his mouth crushed against hers. His kiss was ardent and unrestrained, and Jenna felt as if something wild in both of them had suddenly been set free.

He nipped at her lips, plunged his tongue deeply into the soft recesses of her mouth to taste and explore, and she opened herself to his plundering, her pulse thudding erratically. She was vaguely aware of the sweet tang of apple juice on his lips as she arched her spine, pressed her full, aching breasts against his chest.

Gage kissed her mouth, her cheek, her jaw, smoothed his hands over her back, kneaded her buttocks, pulling her to him where she felt the hard steel of his desire pressing against her belly.

His throaty groan left her breathless, panting, and she felt as if they were running, rushing toward some amazing precipice. She wanted to slow down, to relish every second of the journey, but something inside—some yearning, some insistent and unrelenting need—pushed her ever onward.

Even as they continued to kiss and nuzzle each other, Gage picked her up in his arms and carried her out of the kitchen. She was vaguely aware of passing through the dining room, the living room and the hallway.

She knew they had entered his bedroom from the clean, masculine scent that belonged only to Gage.

While she was still in his arms, she gave into a temptation that had niggled at her for a long time; she combed her fingers through the length of his hair, reveling in its silky texture and discovering that its coolness was so at odds with the sear of his lips against her flesh.

Gage set her down. Obviously impatient now, he pulled her nightgown up her body and over her head, flinging it to some far corner of the room. His dark gaze burned with craving and Jenna loved the idea that she was the one who had induced that glorious expression on his taut features.

Taking her hand, he led her to the bed. He threw back the coverlet and top sheet, and the mattress depressed with their weight as they laid down, side by side.

He kissed and tasted and touched until she was gasping for air, gasping for *him*. She reached up and smoothed her palm over his shoulder, kissed the curve of his corded neck, gently raked her fingernails over his bare back. She tweaked his earlobe between her teeth and grazed the sensitive skin behind his ear with her wet tongue.

He tensed and shivered, drawing his shoulder upward. Then he chuckled suddenly.

Delight rushed through her. "You're ticklish."

He grinned. "Just a little."

He rolled over on top of her then. The sleek curtain of his hair fell across her breasts, the featherlight touch tightening her nipples into nubs. She looked into his eyes, saw that he was staring at her breasts, saw that he wanted to taste her. She arched her back, lifting herself closer to him.

"Please," she whispered, unbothered by her own plaintive mew.

Tentatively, he lowered his head. His mouth was hot and wet as he laved first one breast, then the other. Jenna felt a distinct pulsing at her very center, a moist throbbing sensation that increased with each kiss, each touch, each taste. She closed her eyes, feeling wonderful, feeling *delirious*.

Desire coursed though her body, through her being. She wanted this man. Wanted him more than she had ever wanted anything in her entire life. She wanted all of him. And she wanted it now.

She spoke his name then, and knew that the tremor in her tone conveyed every ounce of the yearning she endured.

He lifted his head and stared into her face, every muscle in his body poised, ready, and Jenna had no doubt that he would satiate her every aching need.

Never for an instant had she lost sight of the significance of this moment. She was about to give herself to a man for the very first time. Instinct told her Gage hadn't been with a woman in many months. Having gotten to know him over the past weeks, she knew he wasn't a man who gave of himself casually. So although their union was an unconventional one at best, their relationship had come to involve a great deal of kindness and caring and trust. The emotions that brought them to this moment were powerful and poignant. And the fact that she was losing her virginity to the man she called her husband filled her with joy.

Hovering over her, he whispered her name, the question in his dark eyes offering her one last chance to put a stop to their lovemaking. But all she could think to do was smile in provocative invitation.

This was what she wanted. Gage was the man she wanted.

And she wanted him now!

Finally, the passion raging through them became overwhelming, and his luscious mouth covered hers at the same instant as he slid himself into her.

Chapter Nine

Jenna awoke with a deep sigh of contentment. She stretched out under the tangle of sheets, loving the feel of the soft, rumpled cotton against her naked skin.

Sunlight streamed through the window, and she smiled. It was going to be a beautiful day.

Rolling over, she experienced a slight pang of disappointment to find that Gage wasn't in the bed next to her. But she thought it was sweet of him to slip away to his work without disturbing her. Although, she wouldn't have minded being disturbed…not if it meant more delicious lovemaking. She grinned. No, she wouldn't have minded that at all!

She relaxed into the pillow, letting her mind drift back. When Gage had first entered her, she'd been seized with a pain that had been sharp enough to widen her eyes. Gage had gone completely still, the passion on his face transforming to surprise as he'd realized that he was her first lover.

For a fraction of a second, she'd feared that the moment was ruined. But she'd reached up, caressed his cheek with her palm and crooned that this was what she wanted. She wanted to surrender her virginity to him. Desire had fogged his black eyes and his lovemaking turned excruciatingly gentle until he had her frantic with need. Her first orgasm had been awesome, as was her second. Jenna grinned wickedly even now in the light of day.

She sat up and listened. The house was quiet, which meant Lily was still asleep. Jenna bounded from bed and raced to her room. She pulled on a fresh pair of panties, a pair of denim shorts and a pink T-shirt. Then she slipped her feet into a pair of canvas sneakers.

In a flash, she'd made a small pot of coffee and was soon carrying two mugs out to the stable.

She found Gage busily brushing one of the horses.

The animal snorted when she entered the stable, and Gage murmured soothingly in its ear. The scent of fresh hay permeated the air.

"Good morning," she called from just inside the door. "Is it okay to come in?"

Gage nodded, but didn't stop attending to the pinto. Jenna couldn't help but notice how Gage's biceps bunched as he ran the bristly brush over the horse's spotted flank.

Having learned over the weeks that it was dangerous to approach the rear of a horse, Jenna eased herself toward the pinto's head and waited for Gage to come to her. When he didn't right away, disappointment made her frown.

"I brought you some coffee."

"Don't want any, thanks."

The crease between her eyes deepened. "What's wrong?" she asked.

"Nothing's wrong." He didn't look at her, but focused his brush strokes on the pinto's rear leg.

In his bent position his hair fell over his shoulders in a black drape. Instantly, Jenna was back in Gage's bed, his hair teasing her flesh like a gossamer curtain. She blinked to dispel the memory and twisted to set the mugs down on a nearby railing.

"Of course, something's wrong. I'm not an idiot. Look at me, Gage. *Talk* to me."

He straightened then, his hand lowering to his side. Clear annoyance flashed in his dark eyes.

When he didn't speak, she said, "This isn't how you greet someone with whom you've just—" she felt the need to choose her words carefully "—been intimate."

Confusion scrambled her thoughts. She'd come out here expecting…what? A warm embrace? A seductive kiss?

Yes, *dammit!* That was exactly what she'd expected. Having been met with his glaring indifference was baffling.

"So you think sex is going to change everything between us."

It wasn't a question, but a statement. And although she was still uncertain about what he was trying to imply—what it was that had him so apathetic—she didn't like his tone at all.

He stalked past her and hung the brush on a hook on the wall with more force than was necessary. "It changes nothing." He gazed off, raking his fingers through his hair. "Who the hell am I kidding? It changes everything."

Jenna wanted to reach out to him. He was close enough that she could feel the warmth of his body, smell the clean, warm scent of him, but some quiet voice deep inside told her it would be unwise to touch him. He wasn't indifferent about what had happened between them; he was cross.

He stepped around her, clicked his tongue and the horse started for the door. As the animal passed, Gage swatted its flank and said, "Go," and the pinto trotted out into the sunny paddock.

Keeping her tone as calm as possible, Jenna asked, "Why are you angry with me this morning?"

"I'm not angry with you." He walked several steps away from her, then turned to face her. "I'm angry with myself." Strain made his features go taut.

"But why?"

"I'm a cheat," he said. "And a thief. I stole your virginity."

Without hesitation, she softly replied, "You can't steal what was freely given."

Simple logic, however, wasn't enough to cool his irritation. Suddenly, it seemed as if he had more energy than he could contain. He paced two steps in one direction, then two steps back. "I've spent the past year feeling cheated. And now—" he raised his palm and slapped it against his chest "—*I'm* the cheater."

Jenna knew his blurted statement was important, but before she could put the pieces together, he continued his rant.

"The Great Spirit stole my family. Left me here alone." He averted his gaze to the far wall. "And this woman is thrust into my life. A woman who not only kept me from finding the release meant for me the day of that damned storm, but who forced her way into my home. Into my life. Who seduced me with her flashing eyes. Her gorgeous body. I'm only human. I'm just a man."

He talked about her as if she were someone else. Some third party they were discussing. But they weren't talking about someone else. It was *her!*

Gage seemed to refuse to meet her gaze. And after all the things he'd said, that infuriated her. If he intended to blame her for the state of his life, the least he could do was look at her.

"So you feel that this is all my fault?" Her volume tipped upward and slight sarcasm laced the question. "You feel that I'm responsible for the fact that we made love last night?"

"We didn't make love," he countered. "We had sex."

Humiliation made her face flame red-hot. She wanted to shout at him. She wanted to rail and scream. But she didn't. She was too mortified to speak.

Why should it bother her how he chose to describe what had happened between them? It shouldn't. It wasn't as if she'd expected last night to transform their empty vows or change their meaningless marriage into something real.

She swallowed, but her throat was so dry that the action actually hurt. The overwhelming shame his curt, tactless opinion of their intimacy caused her was significant.

No man could trigger this kind of indignity, this kind of pain unless she felt something for him. Something deep. Something significant.

Jenna shoved the notion from her mind. Now was *not* the time for her to evaluate her feelings for Gage Dalton.

"What we experienced last night," she snapped, "was beautiful. And I refuse to allow you to cheapen that. Okay, so you don't agree that we made love." She shrugged. "So you want to call it sex. Fine. But whatever name you choose to put to it doesn't change the fact that it was wonderful."

Regret etched into the hard planes of his handsome face, and that only stirred her fury all the more.

"I can't believe," she barreled ahead, full steam, "that you're still bitter that I saved your lousy neck. That I kept you from driving into that flood on Reservation Road. How stupid can you be?"

Whatever remorse might have flitted through him vanished as her insult evidently took hold. His eyes narrowed in what she took to be a warning, but she didn't even consider heeding it.

"Have you stopped for one minute to think—" she tilted her head slightly "—that it wasn't me who saved you that day? But that it was Kit-tan-it-to'wet? That the Great Spirit had a plan that you never imagined?"

His fury was back on full throttle. He didn't have to say anything for her to know it. She could *feel* it.

Before he could respond, she said, "Relief from grief doesn't have to mean the end of one's life, Gage. But it *would* mean the end of life as you know it. Relief could come in the form of a new life—a *new* love."

Embarrassment flashed through her when she saw his jaw tick. Pressing her palm to her chest, she rushed to clarify, "Not necessarily me. That's not what I'm suggesting. But the Great One could bring you a woman to love, Gage. A woman who could make all the hurt and grief disappear. If you could just open yourself up to the idea and let it happen."

For a long moment, silence reverberated off the walls of the stable. Oh, there was sound—birdsong coming from the trees outside, the soft snorts and occasional whinny of the horses that remained in their stalls. But the silence between the two of them was deafening.

Finally, Gage said, "My heart is too frozen to feel love."

Frustration made Jenna clench her teeth. "I wouldn't be surprised to learn that you don't even have a heart."

She felt so hurt and so angry that she found it difficult to take a breath. Apparently, he'd succeeded in reining in his emotions. He stood there looking arrogant and unmoved. How could he be so unresponsive when he'd hurt her with words that had been as sharp as a well-honed ax?

She'd done her best to make him understand that life

had much to offer. Love. Joy. Hope. A future. But he refused to see it.

Oh, she realized that he was blinded by the guilt he wore like a heavy wool coat. That he was left in the land of the living while his wife and daughter had died.

It seemed that his grief was so high he couldn't climb over it, and so wide he couldn't see around it. If he wanted to live the remainder of his days alone and lonely, who was she to tell him he couldn't?

"I'm leaving," she announced. "I'm packing up our things. Lily and I will be gone before the day is over."

She turned and walked toward the door.

"But you can't go."

Jenna turned, her brows raised. "Oh?"

"Have you forgotten about the Council? You can't take Lily off Broken Bow. Not without their permission, anyway."

Right now, she didn't want *anyone* telling her what she could or couldn't do.

"Just let them try to stop me." She turned back toward the doorway and took a single step…and that was all the time it took for her to remember. Hoo'ma. Chee'pai. The rest of the Elders. The entire reservation of Lenape who were striving to preserve the treasure that was their heritage.

How could she disrespect their efforts by walking away with Lily when they truly felt the baby was part of their family?

She couldn't.

Her shoulders rounded in defeat and she reached up to smooth her fingers across her forehead, marveling

that she'd actually succeeded in making this complicated and messy situation more complicated and messy.

She turned to Gage and sighed. Subdued now, she
said, "I'll request a meeting with the Council. But rest
assured, I won't be under your roof come nightfall."

Jenna spooned oatmeal into Lily's mouth, swiped
the baby's chin with a napkin and then looked across the
table at Arlene. "Thanks for letting us stay with you last
night," she told her friend.

They were eating breakfast at Hannah's restaurant
just down the street from Arlene's house. Having barged
in on Arlene yesterday afternoon, Jenna had invited her
to breakfast at the diner with the hope of offering the
woman a small treat as a show of appreciation for her
generous hospitality.

There had been another reason Jenna wanted to go
out to eat. As a diversion for Lily. It seemed the toddler was feeling out of sorts. Jenna feared it was because she was missing Gage. Lily and Gage had
developed a surprisingly close bond over the past
weeks. The baby seemed to sense when he was about
to come in from the stable for the evening, and Lily's
bedtime ritual included a hug and a kiss from Gage.
She'd had trouble falling asleep last night and had
awoken several times during the night. Jenna felt badly
that yet another person was being yanked out of Lily's
life, but for the life of her she didn't know how it could
be helped.

"It's no problem," Arlene said. "You know that. You
and Lily are welcome to stay for as long as you need."

Hannah moseyed over to their table and refilled her mother's coffee cup. She looked at Jenna, lifting the pot. "More?"

"Please." Jenna slid the cup and saucer toward Hannah, but was careful to keep well out of Lily's reach.

"I'm sorry you and Gage are having trouble," Hannah said casually.

"I'm afraid this is more than trouble," Jenna admitted. "I won't be going back there."

Arlene reached across the table to pat Jenna's hand. "Don't say that. The two of you might be able to work things out."

Jenna loved having the support of friends. It made her feel less alone.

She shook her head. "I don't think that will be possible. Gage has…"

Issues was the word she was going to use, but she left it unsaid. Yes, he was living with a tremendous amount of guilt. Yes, he refused to see the future as the bright hope it was meant to be. But it was the fact that he refused to open his heart to love that was going to make it impossible for Gage to ever find happiness. That was the overwhelmingly sad fact of the matter.

The door of the diner opened and Gage strolled in. Something amazing happened to Jenna's entire body. She tingled. All over. He looked so good standing there in his tight T-shirt and form-fitting jeans. His long hair was loose, his black eyes intense.

She did a quick emotional assessment. Did he look as if he'd slept well? Was he worried? Upset?

Jenna knew she shouldn't care. But she did.

Holy heaven! She *was* in love with the man.

She'd suspected it yesterday when he'd cut her to the bone with his angry words and blame. She'd considered the notion again last night when she'd lain in that lonely bed at Arlene's house, her mind incapable of thinking about anything but Gage. And she'd nearly come to the fearful conclusion this morning when she awoke from a vivid, extremely erotic dream featuring Gage.

But each time the suspicions would creep in, she'd done her best to shut them out. However, there was no sense denying reality when it was staring her right in the face.

She loved Gage Dalton. Every thought in her head, every cell in her body was screaming the truth.

"Hi there, Gage," Hannah greeted. "Would you like a cup of coffee?"

"Yes, please," he said, but his eyes never left Jenna. "But I'll take it to go, Hannah, if you don't mind. I've got work waiting for me at home."

He strode across the diner toward Jenna's table.

Arlene murmured, "Maybe I should excuse myself. Give you two some privacy."

"Don't you move," Jenna warned, tossing the woman a quick, narrow-eyed glance.

The instant Lily realized Gage was nearby, she clapped her hands and then raised her arms toward him. As though it was second nature, Gage reached out and plucked the toddler from the high chair.

"Morning, sunbeam," he said. Lily wrapped her small arms around his neck and stole a hug. For an instant, Gage looked as if he was in paradise.

Holding the toddler in one arm, he directed his attention to Jenna. "Good morning."

She nodded a silent greeting.

Arlene slid her chair out. "I need to visit the ladies' room," she said in a rush. "Sit down, Gage." Avoiding Jenna's eyes, Arlene added, "I'll be back in a sec."

Traitor, Jenna wanted to call after her.

Gage remained standing. "I found this at the house." He held up a blue stuffed toy elephant that was one of Lily's favorites. "I thought Lily might miss it."

Jenna had been so focused on his handsome face that she hadn't even noticed he'd been carrying the animal. Lily giggled, accepting the toy from Gage as if it were a brand-new plaything.

What Lily misses, Jenna wanted to say, *is you.* But voicing that thought would be pure foolishness. He'd made his feelings clear. Having Jenna and Lily at the ranch only churned up Gage's guilt. Made him angry enough to lash out at Jenna. She refused to subject herself or the baby to that.

"Thank you." So he wouldn't misinterpret her expression of gratitude, she added, "I'm sure Lily appreciates your bringing her elephant to her."

With the baby's attention on the stuffed animal, tension seemed to settle over Jenna and Gage. He shifted his weight on his feet. She had to concentrate to remain still. Clearly, they were both discomfited.

Finally, he asked, "Were you able to schedule a meeting with the Elders?"

She nodded. "But not until tomorrow. Hoo'ma said

one of the Council members is out of town. They agreed to see me at two o'clock tomorrow afternoon."

"Would you like me to be there?"

The offer startled her. "Why?" The question tumbled off her tongue before she could stop it. Without allowing him to answer, she said, "No, I don't think that will be necessary."

"Okay. Whatever you want."

Oh, no, she thought. That statement was dead wrong.

Strain pulled the air taut again. Gage transferred Lily to the crook of his opposite arm.

"After I tend the horses this morning," he said quietly, "I've got to drive into Billings to meet a client. I won't be home all afternoon. So if you want to come out to the ranch to work, you're welcome to."

Jenna had left her computer at Gage's house, telling him she'd come for it when she and Lily were settled.

"Thanks," she told him. "I might do that."

It felt as if the atmosphere grew weighted.

"Well, if there's nothing else..." He paused. "I guess I'll be going."

But he didn't go, and Jenna couldn't help but think he had something more to say. Or that he suspected she had more to say and he wanted to give her every chance to say it. Well, she'd said everything that had been on her mind. Yesterday.

Gage kissed Lily on the forehead, then gently handed her over to Jenna and turned away from them. He stopped at the register long enough to pay Hannah for his coffee, and then he left the diner.

Nerves twittered in the pit of Jenna's belly to the point that she actually felt queasy. She watched the small group of Elders enter the room and take their seats at the head table.

Through the whole ordeal of facing the deaths of Amy and David, of uprooting herself in order to take care of her niece, Jenna had learned just how strong she was. Oh, she had grieved. However, she'd managed her grief well, she believed. As well as grief could be managed, anyway. She even felt that she'd risen above her anguish in order to create a loving and nurturing environment for Lily. But it would be foolish for her to think she had overcome all her vulnerabilities. The Council members casually chatting at the front of the hall had the power to turn her world upside down again. Jenna truly feared the Elders' response when she told them that she and Gage had separated.

Would they take the baby from her?

The silent question scared her so badly, she could scarcely put two coherent thoughts together. She would not allow anyone to come between her and her niece.

Being the oldest member of the Council, Hoo'ma opened the meeting with a formal greeting, and then asked everyone to bow their heads in prayer as she asked the Great One to be with them and help them in their job of guiding the tribe.

"As all of you know," Hoo'ma addressed the group, "Jenna Dalton has asked to meet with us today." The old woman directed her dark gaze to Jenna. "This is a small community, and news travels faster than the wind. Many of us are aware that you and Lily are staying with Arlene Johnson. We are grateful to you for asking to meet with us. Gossip and innuendo are terrible things, like mean floodwaters that eat away the soil from around a tree's roots. Eventually, even the mightiest oak will fall.

"In light of the situation we are in," Hoo'ma continued, "I hope that you have come here to put an end to hearsay by letting us know exactly what is taking place."

Were it not for the deep concern and obvious support shadowing the woman's gaze, Jenna would have had trouble maintaining eye contact with Hoo'ma. For some reason, her earlier-than-expected separation from Gage made Jenna feel as if she'd failed everyone on the Council. Nerves dried out her lips and she skimmed her tongue along them, and then balled her fists anxiously.

Jenna looked down the row of Lenape Elders. She saw a wide variety of emotions reflected in their faces: doubt, disappointment, curiosity, encouragement and regret. Chee'pai's expression could only be described as smug. But Jenna refused to let the shaman intimidate her.

"I have learned a lot," she began, "during the month I have lived on Broken Bow Reservation. First and foremost, I've learned something about honorable behavior. I've discovered that the Lenape cherish honor almost above all else. And that's why I'm here. I want to be honorable. I want to be forthright about what's happening in my life. And in the life of my niece." Panic shimmered through her. "I hope all of you will bear with me for a moment and take that into consideration after you hear what I have to say."

Jenna sensed that some of the members relaxed, if their nods were any indication. She took a deep breath.

"It is with a very heavy heart," she said, "that I come here to tell you that Gage Dalton and I can no longer remain married." Without thought, she laced her fingers, one thumb worrying back and forth across the other. "What happened between us is personal, and I ask that you respect our privacy. But…because this affects Lily and where she'll be living, I wanted to come here and discuss things with you, and assure you—"

"Where *will* the two of you be living?" Predictably, the blunt interruption came from Chee'pai. Accusation singed the edges of the question.

Jenna had thought she could offer to live with Lily on the rez. But doing so would be terribly difficult for her now that she'd realized her love for Gage. He made her feel like no other man had ever made her feel. However, even though she recognized that fact, she also knew that Gage would never be able to return the love she felt for him.

Living at Broken Bow would remind her of him every single day.

"I'd like to take Lily back to my hometown. Rock Springs." She quickly blurted, "With your permission, of course."

"We will never grant permission for that," Chee'pai declared.

One of the other Council women leaned forward. "With all due respect to our shaman, one person cannot speak for the entire group."

"I agree," a male Council member said, nodding.

"But just a month ago," another man pointed out, "she agreed she would not take the baby from Broken Bow."

"Rock Springs isn't that far away," Jenna pointed out.

Hoo'ma raised her hand and everyone went silent. "As concerned as I am with Lily," the woman said softly, "I am also concerned, Jenna, with your relationship with Gage. I understand that your private life should remain private. But it is only with an open heart that I ask if you're sure the two of you made every attempt to make your relationship work. You have been married such a short time. It is difficult for two people just starting out to—"

"They were not married," Chee'pai blurted.

Shocked, Jenna jerked to face him. "Of course we were married. You saw the license yourself."

Several Council members frowned, and it was clear they were wondering what the shaman might know. Jenna wondered the same thing. Ice-cold trepidation slithered up her spine, and she warded off a shiver.

Chee'pai narrowed his charcoal eyes at her, a clear challenge tightening his expression. "You say you have learned about honor. Can you stand there before this Council and honestly say that you love my grandson?"

Jenna's heart pounded against her ribs. She'd expected to discuss her niece with the Elders today. It had never occurred to her that they would ask personal questions about her relationship with Gage.

She didn't like being put on the spot. Chee'pai had been against her from day one. Suddenly, she wanted more than anything to put him in his place. But doing so would mean she would have to reveal some very privileged information about herself and her feelings.

She squared her shoulders and tipped up her chin. Privacy be damned!

"I can," she told him boldly. "I can stand here and pledge to you and the rest of the Elders that I love Gage Dalton with every ounce of my being."

There! The truth was out. And it did her soul good to see the shaman's superior smirk slip just a notch.

"Jenna." Hoo'ma rested her thin arms on the edge of the long table. "If what you say is true…is there anything we can do to help you and Gage to work things out?"

The thought of Gage sent pain spearing through Jenna. She frowned, trying to figure out how to answer the woman's question. She wished there was something they could do. But there wasn't.

Gage was trapped. Held down by a past mired in grief and guilt. Jenna had tried to free him. She'd tried to make him envision an optimistic future. But he was wearing blinders, it seemed. She couldn't fix this for him.

She felt badly for Gage. Her heart ached for him, for his inability to move forward, but she was determined to do what was best for Lily. To make a hopeful future for her niece. And if that meant letting go of what she couldn't fix, then so be it.

Finally, she shook her head. "I appreciate your concern, your willingness to help. But there's nothing anyone can do."

That was all she intended to say on the subject.

What had taken place between her and Gage was their business.

She stood tall. "I want you to know that I'll do everything in my power to see to it that Lily's life is steeped in Lenape culture. I'll bring her to the reservation often. We'll attend the celebrations and festivals. I truly want her to be a part of this community. To be a part of this family. As she gets older, I promise to—"

"You're lying," Chee'pai said, slapping the table sharply with his palm. "We cannot believe anything that you say."

Hoo'ma's normally calm demeanor cracked. "Chee'-pai, I will not permit this rudeness."

The shaman's haughtiness had returned full force. "I know she is lying. Because Gage told me their marriage was not a love match. He called their marriage an arrangement, and that is proof that the union was not based on the foundation Jenna is claiming."

Jenna was unable to stop her ragged gasp. She'd never felt so betrayed. Yes, she and Gage had experienced bumpy moments over the weeks she'd lived in his home, but she'd thought they had at least become friends. She'd never expected him to reveal the truth about their marriage bargain to his grandfather.

"And if she would lie to us about her marriage to my grandson," Chee'pai said, "then she'll lie to us about her plans for the baby. Lily Collins belongs here. On Broken Bow. Among her Lenape family."

The room went eerily quiet.

Hoo'ma, whom Jenna had felt certain she had won

over, now looked at her with grave doubt. The other
Council members gazed at her, their suspicion evident.

Fear crept over Jenna. A fear that was as bleak and
cold as the dead of winter.

"May I approach the Council table?"

The sound of Gage's voice had Jenna whipping
around. His handsome features looked set in stone as he
walked from the back of the room.

How long had he been there? How much had he
heard? Had he witnessed her profession of love?

The questions made her dizzy. But then anger took
hold.

The person coming toward her had abandoned her.
He'd broken both her faith and her trust. He had di-
vulged their secret when he knew full well that doing
so would cost her custody of Lily.

The fury inside her burned white-hot.

Then she noticed that he looked angry, too.

"What are you doing here?" she said, her voice grating. "I told you not to come."

He brushed past her and stalked toward the Elders,
stopping in front of his grandfather. "I ask for permission to speak."

Chapter Ten

"Of course, Gage," Hoo'ma said gently. "Let me welcome you on behalf of the Council. I think it's safe to say that we'd all be pleased to hear whatever it is you wish to tell us."

Before Gage could speak, Chee'pai said, "Yes, Gage, tell us the truth. All of us are eager to know. Did you marry Jenna out of choice?"

Although his back was to Jenna, Gage could feel her gaze boring into him. Lying to the Elders would be an egregious disrespect. A black mark on his character and his soul.

But he'd come today to do the right thing. Because since meeting Jenna, he'd done everything wrong. Everything.

The knowledge that he'd stolen her virginity still

wrenched his gut. As did the knowledge that he'd upset her so terribly, she'd had to pack up and leave. She deserved so much better than what he'd been able to offer her over the weeks they had pretended to be husband and wife. And he intended to give her what she deserved now.

"Back in the spring," Gage began, "on the day of the terrible storm that caused all the flooding, Jenna and I met on Reservation Road. She stood in the pouring rain, risking her own safety to stop me from driving into the floodwaters that had washed out the roadway. She saved my life. I owed her a Life Gift. So when she came to me looking for help in gaining custody of her niece, I felt I had to help her."

"You had no choice but to repay your debt," Hoo'ma supplied, nodding her head in emphatic defense.

Gage offered the woman a small smile of appreciation. The truth of the matter was he felt sick that he was revealing the secret pact he'd made with Jenna. He hated that he was breaking the promise he'd made to her, but he felt he had no other choice. His grandfather was bent on using the information against her. Half truths were more dangerous than straightforward fact.

Chee'pai's chin tilted in triumph. His gaze swung to Jenna. "So you lied to this Council when you said that you and Gage were in love."

Astonishment made Gage turn and stare at Jenna, but her eyes were riveted to the shaman. Having arrived just as his grandfather accused Jenna of lying about their marriage and about her plans to teach Lily her native culture, Gage had heard her mention nothing of love. He couldn't believe Jenna would tell the Elders—

"You're putting words in my mouth," Jenna charged. "I mean no disrespect, but that's not what I said, Chee'pai. I cannot and would not ever attempt to speak for Gage. I can only speak for myself. And what I told you was the truth."

Gage's lips parted as his jaw went slack. Jenna hadn't mentioned the word love, but his grandfather had. However, Jenna just professed to telling the truth. His mind raced to put it together.

"But that doesn't excuse the fact," Chee'pai said, "that you intentionally manipulated this Council for your own gain."

"I did it for Lily!"

The desperation in Jenna's tone was like a kick to the seat of Gage's pants. He whirled on his heel and faced his grandfather. "Repaying a Life Gift was not the only reason I agreed to help Jenna," he declared.

A deep frown bit into Chee'pai's brow.

"The story Jenna explained," Gage continued, "shocked me. She is Lily's aunt. She is Lily's family. Yet she was not being considered as the child's guardian."

"Of course she was being considered, Gage," Hoo'ma said.

"Honestly?" he asked the woman. "Then why was she given such a runaround? She met with you for weeks and weeks. Provided all the information you asked for. And the members of this Council kept putting more and more roadblocks in her way."

Hoo'ma's lips flattened, and she glanced toward Chee'pai.

The shaman squared his shoulders. "Gage, you know that we must do all we can to preserve our tribe. Lily is Lenape. We felt it was important that she stay here. Among her people."

Gage sighed. "I understand," he said, his tone soft now, "that your intentions are only for the good of the tribe. I attempted to explain that to Jenna. But it seems to me, Grandfather, that the goal has somehow become more important than the people.

"Your inflexibility in wanting to keep the tribe together has alienated people. My parents are two prime examples. Because they wish to live in Arizona—for my mother's health—you have made them feel ostracized. And you denigrate the young people who move from Broken Bow in order to find work, to travel the world, to educate themselves, to experience life. Just because our brothers and sisters, our mothers and fathers feel the need to leave the rez for one reason or another does not make them any less a part of our family. It does not make them any less Lenape."

Gage noticed that his grandfather's body tensed with disapproval, but that didn't thwart him from speaking his mind.

"Granted," Gage continued, "Jenna isn't Indian. But there was a time in Lenape history when the color of a person's skin meant nothing. People of all races and creeds were adopted into the tribe without thought to their outward appearance. French trappers took Lenape wives. Widowed English settlers took Lenape husbands. Orphaned children were taken in, provided for. They all became part of our family. What mattered was the nurturing of the soul. What mattered was that everyone felt wanted and needed and cared for.

"A woman who had maternal feelings for a motherless child would never have been kept from that child for any reason, least of all her ethnicity." Gage glanced at the Elders and understood that all of them knew he spoke the truth.

"Yes—" Chee'pai nodded "—what you say is true. But these are different times. You have to admit that."

Reaching out, Gage rested the fleshy part of his fist on the wooden table. He was very aware of the stillness that had fallen over the room. "All I know is that segregation is an idea that comes from the outside world, not from the Lenape."

Almost simultaneously, the gazes of several of the Elders slid from his.

Gage swung his arm outward to indicate Jenna. "This woman loves that child. She gets up in the night. Makes herself available at all hours. She's put her niece first, taking care of her business only when Lily is napping or sleeping for the night. She worries and frets, cuddles and plays, praises and teaches just as if she were that baby's mother. She couldn't love Lily more had she given birth to her. Jenna uprooted herself at your request. She has made friends here. And not only that, she's gone beyond the call of duty to help the artists of our tribe with the Web site she's building to sell and promote their work. Jenna has an earnest interest in learning our culture so she can teach Lily about her Lenape roots. She deserves to raise that child."

He glanced at Jenna, but she'd dipped her head. He had no way of knowing what she might be thinking.

"I want to urge each and every one of you to—" He stopped suddenly, feeling as if the remainder of his sentence had been choked off. "I want to urge you to—" Again, his request caught, refusing to be uttered.

He swallowed around the knot that had suddenly formed in his throat. What was wrong with him? He'd come here to help her. And that was what he intended to do.

"Please," he said, forcing his tongue to work, "give Jenna your blessing to leave Broken Bow with Lily." His breath went suddenly and surprisingly ragged as he finished, "If that is what she chooses to do."

Jenna was dumbfounded by all that Gage had said. She was utterly amazed that he would even show up here at the meeting after the angry words they had tossed at each other just a couple of days ago. And she was staggered by the arguments he'd made on her behalf, especially since he'd told her from the start that if it was discovered that he had tried to deceive the Elders, he could be ousted from the tribe.

At the same time she felt heartbroken. If he hadn't been standing in the back of the hall to overhear her heartfelt profession to the Elders, then he most certainly deciphered her feelings by what she'd been forced to admit to Chee'pai with Gage standing right there beside her. Yet knowing that he'd captured her heart, Gage had still asked the Council to let her leave Broken Bow with Lily. That was a clear message of just how badly he wanted her gone.

Not that she'd expected anything else. He'd made his feelings obvious when they had argued at the stable. But still, hearing him urging for her release churned up a startlingly strong sadness in her.

She stepped forward to address the Elders. "I should probably apologize to all of you for how I handled things." She paused long enough to take a deep breath. "But I'd be lying if I said I was sorry. About anything."

Although she couldn't bring herself to glance at the man standing next to her, she was keenly aware of the solid mass of him just inches away. But she kept her eyes trained forward. "Had I not met Gage the day of the terrible storm, I would not have had the means to convince the Council to grant me custody of my niece. Had he not opened his home to me here on Broken Bow, I would never have realized the awesome heritage that is an indelible part of who Lily is." She directed her attention to the shaman who seemed to remain in deep contemplation. "Chee'pai, I understand your wanting to hold fast to Lenape traditions. And I want you to know that, no matter where Lily and I end up, I still want her to be a part of this loving family. I would not have been able to say that a month ago. So I can't stand here and apologize for what could be described as my less-than-honorable choices."

Despite sound reason, Jenna found herself turning to face Gage. "I don't regret anything."

If the soft tone of her voice didn't reveal to the Elders the intimate meaning behind her words, then the heat suffusing her face surely would.

With her heart hammering, she lifted her gaze back

toward the Council. "I hope you won't take Lily from me. I love my niece, as Gage said, just as much as if I had given birth to her. I want her with me. I need her with me."

The Council was quiet, clearly pensive. Finally, Hoo'ma spoke. "I think a final vote is in order, but because this is such an important issue—a child's future—I'll ask if there is any further discussion that needs to take place first."

She paused to give the members a chance to speak their minds, and the silence seemed to last an eon for Jenna.

When no one exercised their right to speak, Hoo'ma continued, "No one can predict the future. No one can say what might happen between Gage and Jenna and Lily. The Great One has a way of twisting and shaping tomorrow in ways that none of us ever expect. But whatever fate has in store, I personally believe that Lily Collins should be with Jenna. The child is firmly entrenched in Jenna's heart. Jenna has certainly proved her love for the child. Whether Jenna decides to stay here with us or leave the reservation, I believe mother and child should be together. All who agree please speak up now."

One by one, the Elders made their judgment known by nodding or raising their hands. Chee'pai's brow was puckered and he remained still for the longest time. Finally, he gave a silent nod.

Jenna closed her eyes and released a huge exhalation, her great relief and gratitude lifting her lips in a smile. The Council members rose and rounded the table to offer her congratulatory hugs and handshakes. Gage had stepped aside to let the others come near.

The feelings rolling through her were peculiar; an odd mixture of pleasure and pain. She'd finally achieved her goal of becoming Lily's formal guardian. But she felt like a completely different person now. Her weeks at Broken Bow—living as Gage's wife—had changed her.

After saying her goodbyes, she found herself searching the room for Gage once again. He was enmeshed in an intense conversation with Hoo'ma and another Council member.

Jenna owed him a great deal. Without his help, without his zealous plea, she knew the Council never would have granted her custody. She wanted desperately to thank him. But knowing how he felt about her, about how difficult their act of intimacy had been for him to deal with, she decided to make their final parting as easy on him as possible. Without another word, she simply slipped away.

"Gage, could we talk?"

His grandfather's question made Gage pause just as he was about to pull open the door of his pickup. He'd kept silent about his grandfather's stubborn attitude for far too long, and Gage didn't mind facing Chee'pai now that he'd had the chance to speak his mind. However, now wasn't a good time.

"It will have to be later, Grandfather," he said. "I have to—"

"Please. I have a couple of things I need to say."

Entreaty etched the deep lines in the old man's face, and Gage released his hold on the door handle of the truck.

"I realize," Chee'pai said, "that I have been...mulish in my thinking. But I hope you understand that I only had the best of intentions."

Gage nodded. "I do know that."

"You see, inside me there is a vicious battle going on. Two wolves are fighting. One represents my love for my family—you, your father and mother, and the others here on Broken Bow. The other represents my need to keep our heritage burning so bright that it will shine far into the future."

The small muscles around Gage's mouth softened. He knew that even though his grandfather was a hard man, his objective was pure.

"I understand," Gage assured him.

"I was proud of you in there. All the things you said to the Elders today were true. And I wanted to thank you for reminding me that the Lenape way is to be open and accepting of others and their needs. Holding on to tradition is good and right, but not at the expense of those we love. It is a delicate balance. I appreciate your wisdom in helping me steady the scales."

The rare compliment filled Gage with pride.

"Would you give me your parents' phone number?" his grandfather asked. "I'd like to call my son and his wife. To say hello. To ask them how they are doing." He grinned. "And when they intend to visit this old man."

A smile curled Gage's lips. "They would love to hear from you." He embraced his grandfather and felt his heart pinch with warmth.

When they parted, Chee'pai tilted his head a fraction. "You need to know that you have a fierce wolf war going on inside you, too, Grandson."

Gage had no clue what to call the chaotic mess churning inside his chest, but Chee'pai had offered a pretty accurate description.

"I can feel your conflict," his grandfather continued. "I believe that one of your wolves is staunchly struggling to keep the past alive." He paused, then added, "The other is fighting for the future."

Chee'pai had trained as the tribe's shaman because he had shown incredible intuitive abilities. Gage was discovering just how perceptive his grandfather could be.

"You know in your heart that you cannot live in the past, Grandson. And you have deep feelings for Jenna. Even an old fool like me can see that. She brought you back to the land of the living. Please stay with us. Those who have crossed to the other side would want that for you." Chee'pai grasped Gage's shoulder and gave it a comforting squeeze. "Yet, I also understand the importance of keeping the memory fires burning. Deciding which is most crucial—the past or the future—is a dilemma for us all."

Dilemma? And here Gage had thought he'd reached an impossible impasse where his emotions were concerned. He had come to care for little Lily. Enjoyed being with her. And Jenna! His feelings for Jenna were all-encompassing. He'd enjoyed the family unit the three of them made. But each time he contemplated the situation, his conscience never failed to lapse into deep remorse. He felt guilty contemplating a future with Jenna and Lily, a future filled with happiness, when Mary Lynn and Skye weren't here to share in it.

Gage murmured, "And the war wages on." Straightening his spine, he lifted his anguished gaze to his grandfather's. "You are a wise man. A man who sees things that are invisible to others. I need you to tell me. Which wolf inside me will win?"

A deep abiding love misted Chee'pai's eyes as he said, "The one you feed."

Jenna was crouched beneath the desk unplugging the computer and monitor from the electrical outlet. After stopping at Arlene's to give her the good news that the Elders had granted her full custody of Lily, Jenna had asked her friend if she could keep the baby for just a little while longer so she could drive out to Gage's house to pick up her belongings. She'd hoped against hope that she could arrive at the ranch, gather the remainder of her things and leave before Gage returned.

She didn't want to cause him any more heartache.

Unbidden, an image flashed into her brain of the two of them arguing in the stable the morning after they'd made love. True torment had shadowed his eyes, rounded his muscular shoulders.

At first, she'd felt angry with him. How dare he take the beautiful moments they had shared together and turn them into something ugly. Something dark.

As she'd seen it, nothing shameful had taken place between them that fateful night. In fact, the intimacy they had shared had been glorious. Like nothing she'd ever experienced.

And she'd quickly discovered why, too. She'd fallen in love with the man.

Love meant many things—sharing a warm summer's

night, laughing together, kissing, touching, making love. And maybe she wore rose-colored glasses, but, to her, love meant something else, as well. It meant doing all in your power not to hurt the one you adore, and that was what she was doing right now.

Working swiftly, she unhooked the wires for the keyboard, monitor and speakers from the computer's tower.

Then she pulled one end of the phone cord from the outlet on the wall, and the other from the socket on the tower. She coiled it into a neat bundle.

Gathering up all the wires and cords, she backed out from under the desk on her hands and knees. The sound of the front door made her scramble a little more quickly.

"Jenna."

Instinct had her turning toward the sound of Gage's voice and her head thudded softly against the underside of the desk.

She leaned back on her heels, pressing her palm to the back of her skull. Gage squatted next to her.

"Are you okay?" he asked.

Jenna nodded. "I'd hoped to get my computer and get out of here before you returned home."

She tried to keep her eyes trained on the floor, but the sight of him was too much of a temptation. Her gaze rose to his jean-clad thighs. His palms were splayed there, and she remembered how urgent his touch had been when they'd made love. Jenna moistened her lips and tipped up her chin, taking in his trim waist, his powerful chest. Their gazes clashed, and she knew without a doubt that she'd never meet another man like him, not even if she searched the whole world over.

His shoulders sagged a fraction as he sighed. "I can't believe what I've done."

The statement confused her.

He stood in one fluid motion, murmuring, "I've fed the wrong wolf."

Gage reached out his hand to her.

"Fed the wrong…" Shaking her head in bewilderment, she slid her palm into his and let him help her to her feet. Acute disappointment flooded her when he released her hand immediately. She reached over and set the coiled telephone cord on the desktop. "What are you talking about?"

"I talked to my grandfather after the meeting."

Jenna glanced at the keyboard. "I can't believe Chee'pai voted to give me custody. I never thought that would happen." She took a deep breath and looked at Gage. "It was you, you know. You convinced him. You convinced them all."

"I only spoke the truth. I've seen you with Lily. You've become her mother."

Her heart warmed. "Thank you, Gage. For everything. I wanted to speak to you after the meeting, to thank you, but…" Chagrin made her pause, but he deserved to know why she hadn't expressed her appreciation. "But I thought you'd rather I come here and clear out for good."

A frown scored his forehead as he said, "I did make you think that, didn't I?"

What an odd question for him to ask. She had no idea how she was supposed to respond or if he even expected her to, so she remained silent.

"I'm as stubborn as Grandfather, Jenna." He ran agitated fingers over the upholstered back of the desk chair that sat close by. "I've said things…done things…"

Jenna went very still.

Gage was silent for several long moments. Finally, he said, "When Mary Lynn and Skye and I were a family, I felt like a towering ponderosa pine. Strong. Lush. And forever green, alive. I was happy. I thought nothing could touch us. But the accident…the accident cut me deep. Cut me clean in two. And in an instant, there was nothing left of me but a dead stump. And I stayed that way for months and months and months."

He reached out. Hooked his little finger with hers.

"Then you came along," he said. "You brought sunshine with your nurturing ways. With your laughter. With your kindness and concern. And the roots of my soul sent out new shoots and branches and leaves." Gage smiled. "I'm alive again, Jenna. Because of you."

"B-but…you said—"

Gage leaned forward and gently touched his index finger to her lips. "Shhh, please don't remind me of how stupid I've been." He heaved a sigh. "I wasn't happy to have you here when you first moved in, you know that's true. I was afraid. Afraid that having Lily in the house would churn up bad memories for me. But what I realized was that spending time with her made me remember wonderful moments that I'd spent with Skye. Moments that had been buried under a thick blanket of grief.

"But the worst thing I felt," he continued, "was the guilt of wanting you."

Jenna would have been lying if she said she didn't feel just a little vindicated by his admission. That he wasn't placing all the blame of what happened between them on her shoulders.

"The morning I woke up with you in my bed—" he closed his eyes for a moment and shook his head back and forth "—it was horrible, Jenna. And when you came out to the stable and we argued…everything you said was the truth. But I was too enveloped in darkness to admit it. I couldn't seem to find a way to hold on to the memories of a past I cherished and reach out to the bright future you represented. And knowing that I had taken your virginity…" He closed his eyes and shook his head again. "I felt I deserved to be horsewhipped, and I was too overwhelmed to think clearly." His tone was soft as he added, "I don't mind telling you, though, that after you packed up and left, this house has never felt so empty.

"I don't want to be empty anymore, Jenna. Not my house. Not my life." He slid his hand into hers. "Not my heart."

The whole while he'd been talking, she felt her chest fill with an airy lightness. She recognized it as hope. Still, she had a question that was burning to be asked.

"What about the guilt you've been feeling? It can't have just dissolved."

He seemed to ponder for several seconds. "I told you I talked to Grandfather. He's been a stubborn man for as long as I can remember. But he told me he's going to call my parents."

"That's wonderful," Jenna said; however, she

couldn't see how his grandfather had anything to do with the two of them.

Gage nodded. "I don't want to wake up one day and realize that I allowed the past to hold me prisoner. I want to let go of my guilt. I want to remember Mary Lynn and Skye because I loved them. And they deserve to be remembered. But I know in my heart that everything happens for a reason. Sometimes events don't seem logical, or even sane, but it's those times that I must remember that Kit-tan-it-to'wet is in control. I don't have to understand it all. But I do have to take part in life. I have to appreciate each glorious day as it comes. And I haven't taken part or appreciated my blessings for a long time."

The hope Jenna felt intensified and grew brilliant.

"We were meant to meet on that rainy road," he said. "That day was the beginning of my rebirth. And I was too blind to see it." He inched closer. "What I'm trying to say, Jenna, is that I love you. I want you. And Lily. Here. With me."

Suddenly, he couldn't meet her gaze, and Jenna smiled at his sudden shyness. Then he looked directly into her eyes.

"Would you think about it?"

Pure joy burst inside her, filling every nook and cranny with wonder and delight. An elated smile spread across her lips.

"Think about it? I don't need to think about anything!" She wrapped her arms around his neck, kissed him on the mouth, on the jaw, on the cheek. "I love you,

Gage Dalton," she whispered in his ear. "And although I have no clue what you meant about feeding the wrong wolf, I fully intend to help you fatten up the right one."

* * * * *

SILHOUETTE *Romance*®

Matilda Grant signed on to a reality
show to win fifty thousand dollars,
but once she met contestant
David Simpson all the rules changed!

Don't miss a moment of

The Dating Game

by

SHIRLEY JUMP

Silhouette Romance #1795

**On sale
December 2005!**

Only from Silhouette Books!

SPECIAL EDITION™

Here comes the bride…
matchmaking down the aisle!

HIS MOTHER'S WEDDING
by **Judy Duarte**

**When private investigator Rico Garcia
arrived to visit his recently engaged
mother, the last thing on his mind was
becoming involved with her
wedding planner.**

**But his matchmaker of a mom
had other ideas!**

*Available January
wherever you buy books.*

Where love comes alive™

If you enjoyed what you just read,
then we've got an offer you can't resist!

Take 2 bestselling
love stories FREE!

Plus get a FREE surprise gift!

Clip this page and mail it to Silhouette Reader Service™

IN U.S.A.	**IN CANADA**
3010 Walden Ave.	P.O. Box 609
P.O. Box 1867	Fort Erie, Ontario
Buffalo, N.Y. 14240-1867	L2A 5X3

YES! Please send me 2 free Silhouette Romance® novels and my free
surprise gift. After receiving them, if I don't wish to receive anymore, I can
return the shipping statement marked cancel. If I don't cancel, I will receive 4
brand-new novels every month, before they're available in stores! In the U.S.A.,
bill me at the bargain price of $3.57 plus 25¢ shipping and handling per book
and applicable sales tax, if any*. In Canada, bill me at the bargain price of $4.05
plus 25¢ shipping and handling per book and applicable taxes**. That's the
complete price and a savings of at least 10% off the cover prices—what a great
deal! I understand that accepting the 2 free books and gift places me under no
obligation ever to buy any books. I can always return a shipment and cancel at
any time. Even if I never buy another book from Silhouette, the 2 free books and
gift are mine to keep forever.

210 SDN DZ7L
310 SDN DZ7M

Name	(PLEASE PRINT)
Address	Apt.#
City	State/Prov. Zip/Postal Code

Not valid to current Silhouette Romance® subscribers.

Want to try two free books from another series?
Call 1-800-873-8635 or visit www.morefreebooks.com.

* Terms and prices subject to change without notice. Sales tax applicable in N.Y.
** Canadian residents will be charged applicable provincial taxes and GST.
  All orders subject to approval. Offer limited to one per household.
  ® are registered trademarks owned and used by the trademark owner and or its licensee.

SROM04R   ©2004 Harlequin Enterprises Limited

SILHOUETTE Romance ®

COMING NEXT MONTH

#1798 LOVE'S NINE LIVES—Cara Colter and Cassidy Caron
PerPETually Yours
Justin West wasn't looking for commitment, but everything about
Bridget Daisy exemplified commitment—especially her large
tabby cat, who seemed to think there was room for only one
male in Bridget's life. Justin couldn't agree more. So he vowed
to be a perfect gentleman. Only problem was he had *never* been
a gentleman....

#1799 THAT TOUCH OF PINK—Teresa Southwick
Buy-a-Guy
Uncertain how to help her daughter win a wilderness survival badge,
Abby Walsh buys ex-soldier Riley Dixon at a charity bachelor
auction. But will their camping trip earn Abby's *romantic* survival
skills merely a badge for courage, or a family man to keep?

#1800 SOMETIMES WHEN WE KISS—Linda Goodnight
Family business might have brought Jackson Kane home after
ten long years but it had always been personal between him and
Shannon Wyoming. Now he was her key to holding on to all that
she held most dear...but what price would she pay for saying
"yes" to his proposal?

#1801 THE RANCHER'S REDEMPTION—Elise Mayr
Desperate to save her sick daughter, widow Kaya Cunningham had no
choice but to return to the Diamond C Ranch and throw herself on the
mercy of her brother-in-law. And though Joshua had every reason to
despise Kaya for the secret she'd kept from his family, his eyes reflected
an entirely different emotion....

SRCNM1205